THE RIYADH CONSPIRACY

a Novel by

Malcolm Mahr

ISBN: 978-0-9830007-8-5

Fiction Publishing, Inc.
Ft. Pierce, Florida 34982
www.fictionpublishinginc.com
fictionpub@bellsouth.net

For Bob Smelkinson and Herb Garten,
for friendship, and as always,
for my wife, Fran,
and my sons, Jamie, Scott and Adam

Also by Malcolm Mahr

FICTION

The Secret Diary of Marco Polo

Murder at the Paradise Spa

The Mystery of DaVinci's Monna Vanna

NONFICTION

How to Win in the Yellow Pages

What Makes a Marriage Work

You're Retired Now. Relax.

THE RIYADH CONSPIRACY

He gathered the kings together unto a place called in the Hebrew tongue Armageddon. And the seventh angel poured out his vial into the air and there came a great voice out of the temple of heaven, from the throne, saying, "It is done."

Revelation 16:16-17

PART I

THE SAMSON OPTION

And Samson grasped the two middle pillars on which the house rested, and braced himself against them, the one with his right hand and the other with his left.

And Samson said, "Let me die with the Philistines!" And he bent with all his might so that the house fell on the lords and all the people who were in it. So the dead whom he killed at his death were more than those whom he killed in his life.

Judges 16:29-30
New American Standard Bible

...Prologue

Jerusalem, Israel
October 27, 1984

THE LOW CLOUDS OVER THE HOLY CITY were drenched in a blood-red saffron light the night Avram Markus deserted the Israeli Army. At the time of the "incident" Captain Markus, a decorated veteran of the elite commando unit Sayeret Matkal, was lecturing on surveillance techniques at the Mossad training academy ten miles north of Tel Aviv in the rocky hillside town of Herzilya. The building housed Israel's foreign intelligence service, referred to as "the Office."

A collective gasp came from the trainees as the Sayeret Matkal brigade commander Ephraim Chpindel and Israeli Prime Minister Yitshak Shamir strode into the classroom. The former underground leader and spymaster Shamir was a squat, powerfully built man of sixty-nine. His hair was the color of steel wool, his eyes dark and forceful.

Avram Markus noted the solemn expressions on both men's faces. He drew quick breaths to steady his heart rate. He had a premonition of death, so clear it felt like a stone lodged in his heart.

Chpindel dismissed the assembled trainees. The brigade commander touched Avram's shoulder gently. He had deep shadows under his moist eyes. "Bad news, I'm afraid."

The prime minister added, "A terrorist attack from a Lebanese Shiite resistance movement calling itself Hezbollah. They ambushed an army patrol in the security zone. Five Lebanese and three of our boys were killed during an exchange of rocket and gunfire along the border." He paused, shaking his head sadly. "It is regrettable, but one of our rockets accidentally fell near the Hezbollah position in Ghajar."

"Ghajar! Sarai and Zak are—" Then he knew why Shamir had come in person. His voice was low and cracked. "My wife and son. Are they—"

Chpindel nodded.

Avram felt the white-hot anger rising within him. "Collateral damage"—that's what the military called civilian deaths.

"We're Sayeret Matkal," he heard Chpindel say. "We mourn our dead and keep them in our hearts. But we must go on with our lives."

"Captain Markus." The prime minister spoke quietly and firmly. "The last thing the country needs at this time is rising worries of a new front heating up in South Lebanon. I must order you not to discuss this unfortunate accident."

"I'll think about it," Avram blurted out. He couldn't breathe. He glared at the Israeli prime minister, his eyes cold and expressionless. A coiled snake in his stomach stirred. Avram knew he had to get away or lose his sanity. The shock of powerlessness, the sickening disgust at the rank injustice that had rained on his innocent wife and son. Desolation turned into rage and despair that led the forty-nine-year-old Avram Markus to desert the Israeli Defense Force, flee the country of his birth, and embark on a violent path that shaped his life.

...1

THE OLD MAN WAS A NIGHT WANDERER. At seventy-six years of age he walked with a pronounced limp and a cane. The Indian River Lagoon waterfront in downtown Fort Pierce was deserted, silent, except for the sound of waves slapping gently on hulls. The sky over the ocean was shadowy black, the air chilly.

Avram Markus had been an asset in the CIA's black operations for twenty-five years, code-named Scorpion. The veteran operative paused; the nape of his neck prickled. Two men emerged from the shadows of the Fort Pierce Branch Library.

"Gotta cigarette, Grandpa?"

The old man shook his head, leaning heavily on his cane and studying the men. The bigger one, a lumbering beefy giant with a porcine face, was wearing baggy jeans and a soiled tee shirt. He was well over six feet tall, with a shaven skull and arms like hams. The second man was shorter, wearing dark pants and a blue zip-fronted windbreaker. His pale gaze was as placid as the other's was threatening. Long hair fell below his ears.

"How can I be of service to you gentlemen?"

"Your watch and wallet, that's how," the beefy one said.

Avram heard the click of a spring-loaded knife snapping open; a glint of metal flashed in the pale yellow dock light. He studied the way the man waved the weapon out in front of him. *Amateurs,* he thought, shifting the cane into his right hand while depressing a button under the cane's handle. A half-inch needle tipped with deadly scorpion venom jutted from the bottom of the cane.

Outnumbered and outweighed, the older man's dredged-up, half-forgotten lethal reflexes started to take over. He willed them in check; he had been around too much death for too many years. Avram took a deep breath and retracted the toxic needle.

"Your wallet," the big man repeated in a threatening tone.

Avram sighed and held out his wallet. Just as the beefy man reached for it, Avram let it tumble from his fingertips. The mugger's eyes moved from Avram to the wallet for an instant. In one fluid motion, the old man whipped his cane sharply against the extended knife arm, causing his surprised assailant to drop the weapon. Then he seemed to sway slightly at the hips, turning his shoulders to add force to the blow as he smashed the cane's metal handle hard against the man's windpipe. The big man staggered back, throwing both hands to his throat. His eyes bulged; gurgling sounds escaped his lips. Choking, unable to breathe, he reeled drunkenly away. The short companion stared in disbelief. Avram took a threatening step toward him, and he disappeared into the dark shadows of the library.

The old man continued his solitary stroll north on Indian River Drive at a leisurely pace so as not to tire his leg. Turning left at Avenue D, he walked one block, stopping at a pastel green two-story clapboard house. He checked the sliver of scotch tape he'd fastened to the top of the doorsill from force of habit. It was intact. A man in his line of work made serious enemies. One day, he was certain, they would come for him.

...2

"WE'LL USE THE RADAR-IMAGING SPYSAT," said Dorothy Schreck, the assistant director of Central Intelligence. Schreck was fifty-five, maybe more, tall and thick and heavy, with steel-gray hair cut short. Her dark eyes were lined with too much makeup. She was unmarried and rarely dated, which had led to persistent speculation among colleagues that she was a lesbian. She added, "Herro Zakariya's debriefing will be transmitted by satellite live from our embassy in Mayfair."

"Who's interrogating this guy?" asked the CIA director. Phillip Gervaise was forty-six years old, trim and good looking, with a perpetual tan and only a touch of gray at the temples. He wore a bow tie because he believed it gave him a professorial look.

"Roland Howard."

"Good. Rocky Howard is a professional."

Schreck checked her watch and clicked on the TV remote. "I also dispatched Agent Khouri as an interpreter if needed. We want no muck-ups in translation."

A voice-over said, "My name is Colonel Roland M. Howard, deputy station chief at the American Embassy, London. The time is 10 a.m. I am debriefing on videotape Herro Zakariya, code name Omar."

On the TV screen a dusty-complexioned man was seated on one side of a wooden table. He wore dark glasses. A surgical mask covered much of his nose and mouth, and a Liverpool Football Club cap was canted over his eyebrows.

"Go ahead," Howard prodded.

Zakariya's scratchy voice spoke tonelessly through a voice altering apparatus. "My name, my voice and my appearance today are

7

disguised to protect my family back in Iran and, more so, to protect the individuals whom I recruited, and who are still working inside the country." He paused, staring uneasily at the TV camera. "From my sources, word has been received that Iran has been successful in enriching weapons grade uranium."

"Where?" Howard interrupted.

"Natanz, Ardakan, and outside the city of Gachin, near the Gulf."

"Continue."

"Last month, Iran received delivery by ship of fully-operational, state-of-the-art missiles. Missile parts were transited by air from North Korea to Beijing, where they were put on Iran Air cargo flights to Tehran."

"What type missiles were delivered?"

"Chinese-made M-9 short-range ballistic missiles capable of carrying nuclear warheads. The M-9 has a range of 600 kilometers. It is equipped with a single warhead that can either be nuclear, high explosive, or chemical. This military hardware is secret and was not on display in the big parade when the Pasdaran—"

Howard broke in. "Who are Pasdaran?"

A soft female voice off-camera explained, "Iran's Revolutionary Guard."

"Fill us in on the Revolutionary Guard... Omar?"

"Since the last election the Pasdaran has assumed a more assertive role in determining national policy. They are under direct control of President Hanoush. You Americans must understand this is a messianic regime. They plan to attack Israel with Russian suitcase bombs and missiles armed with nuclear warheads, then hide in bunkers until their religious prophecy is fulfilled and the Mahdi comes to kill the nonbelievers."

"Who the hell's the Mahdi?" Howard whispered to the woman out of view.

"*Al-Mahdi* is 'the rightly-guided one' who, according to Islamic tradition, will come before the end of time to make the entire world Muslim."

"I can't wait," Howard said, resuming his questioning. "You say Iran is going to attack Israel. How do we know that your claims aren't as phony as Ahmed Chalabi's, who conned us into believing Saddam Hussein had weapons of mass destruction? Are you willing to submit to a polygraph test?"

Beads of sweat formed on the man's furrowed forehead. "I speak only truth. I love America. After the overthrow of the shah, I was enthusiastic about the revolution. I quit my studies and joined the Revolutionary Guard."

Howard sounded skeptical. "You worked in intelligence?"

"Yes, sir. In *Nir-ye Qods*. They are a special unit of the Army of the Guardian of the Islamic Revolution. Our responsibility was missile targeting. I saw what was being planned." He took a deep breath. "I became disenchanted, but I could not quit my post. That action would have endangered my family. Could I have some water, please?"

After a few moments, a beautiful dark-haired lady could be seen reaching across the table and handing Zakariya a glass. Sweat spots were visible under his armpit as he drank the water.

Howard let the silence build. "The lost Russian suitcase bombs are yesterday's news. Most of them have either rusted out or would have been bought on the black market and used by Chechnyans. So, what can you tell us about the missiles that we don't already know?"

Zakariya squirmed visibly. "I told you Iran had possession of the Chinese-made M-9 and the M-11 short-range ballistic missiles. The M-11 has a range of 800 kilometers, which means it could drop a nuclear bomb almost anywhere in Israel—"

"What's the payload?"

"Ten to twenty kiloton nuclear bomb capability."

"What were the targets in Israel?"

"Our instructions were to follow the example of the 9-11 planners: strike the financial center, the military center, and aim for maximum psychological damage."

"Go on."

"Tel Aviv is the economic target." He took another deep breath. "The center of Israel's weapons program is the Negev Nuclear Research Center in Dimona, and Tell El Mutesellim in the Jezreel Valley is the psychological target."

"Why Tell El Mutesellim?"

Again the soft female whisper. "It's Arabic for Megiddo."

Howard shrugged. "Anything else before we wrap up? So far, I'm underwhelmed."

Herro Zakariya took another sip of water. "Fourteen thirty-two," he confided quietly.

"Fourteen thirty-two?"

"On the Islamic calendar, 1432 is the date of *Eid al-Adha*."

"So?"

This time the woman's voice had a note of urgency. "*Eid al-Adha* is an important sacrificial religious holiday for Muslims around the world, commemorating Ibrahim's willingness to slay his son as an act of obedience to God."

Howard groaned. "I don't like where this is headed. When is this *Eid al-Adha*?"

"November 5th."

"That's seven days from now."

At Langley, CIA Director Gervaise said, "I've seen enough. Turn it off. It could be legit, it could be bullshit, could be smoke and mirrors. Have Rocky's people babysit Zakariya; fly him to Langley tomorrow for a full vetting, lie detector, psychological testing, the whole schmear."

Schreck said, "We don't want flack for failing to provide warning of a possible Mideast flare-up. I'll call Campbell, give him a heads-up, and special messenger to him a copy of the Zakariya video along with the classified reports from Jordan's GID, Germany's

Federal Intelligence Service and Pakistan's Inter-Services Intelligence."

Gervaise laughed. "Injun-Joe Campbell is in over his head. This alleged Iranian threat made our new director of national intelligence run to Kemo Sabe Kennan."

...3

THE PHONE BUZZED in Herro Zakariya's room at the Radisson Edwardian Sussex Hotel situated on a quiet corner near Marble Arch in Mayfair, London. Zakariya, code-named Omar, awoke, struggling to focus his eyes on the digital bedside clock. "It's two a.m.," he grumbled.

"These things are best done with no prying eyes," the sexy voice answered in Arabic. "I will be there shortly." Click.

It was 2:07 when the elderly female front-desk clerk glanced at her watch. A fashionably dressed Middle Eastern-looking woman entered the Radisson lobby wearing gloves and toting a large handbag.

"Mr. Omar's room number, please."

"Two-twelve," the night clerk answered with a friendly smile and a wink, thinking, *Mr. Omar has good taste, he does. Expensive, too, I imagine.*

Herro Zakariya heard a gentle tap at his door. He padded over, opened it and smiled as he eyed his visitor. She was tall and slim, with olive-toned skin, oval almond eyes and dark hair tied back. "You have money, passport and ticket?"

The woman stared into his eyes, nodded, and put her fingers to her lips, whispering, "Room may be bugged. Put on the television."

Zakariya flipped on the TV remote and leered at the woman's ample breasts. He pointed to the mini bar. "Champagne?"

She winked, touched her tongue to her lips and handed Zakariya a 15-inch laptop computer. "First business; then pleasure."

"What is this?" he asked, puzzled.

The woman reached into her handbag again, this time removing a 9 mm Beretta with an attached silencer. She fired one quick shot into the Iranian's head and two in his chest. The silenced percussion sounded like pops in the small room.

Zakariya gazed at her with surprise, and then his knees buckled and he fell onto his face. The assassin calmly dipped two gloved fingers into the pooling blood and scrawled on the beige walls, "Death to American spies." She turned off the TV, picked up her spent cartridges, and took one last look around the room to make certain she'd left no trace of herself behind.

As the woman approached the lobby, the night clerk eyed her. "Now that's what I call a quickie," she cackled. "Best button up, dearie, it's getting cold outside."

The assassin flashed the Beretta again, firing two bullets into the old woman's chest. Blood splattered on the creamy-white lobby walls and on the ornate golden Buddha statue of Amitabha standing in the gesture of meditation with palms upwards, shielding the whirring, newly installed lobby security cameras.

The assassin was skilled in the art of moving through city streets unseen. She turned up her coat collar and strolled to the nearest intersection. Her bloody gloves were pitched into a trash bin on Gloucester Street, the gun and cartridges dropped into the water drain on Seymour Street.

Alie Khouri took no pleasure from killing, nor any guilt or remorse. She had been trained by the CIA to carry out assassinations with operational calm and mechanical precision. She wasn't responsible; the people in Washington who ordered the deaths were the real killers. She was the designated weapon. If she had not carried out the assignment, someone else would have. Alie flipped her cell phone open and punched in a preprogrammed number.

...4

A SHEEN OF COLD SWEAT formed on the brow of the director of national security as he reviewed Herro Zakariya's London videotape. Joseph Campbell's expression darkened. His heart gave a sideways lurch. Producing a handkerchief, he mopped his damp forehead and grabbed the phone to alert the president of the United States.

"POTUS is boarding Air Force One," said the head of the Secret Service detail.

"Get the president off the plane; we have a problem."

The man demurred. "He's flying to Hollywood for a major fundraiser."

Campbell barked, "If I am not immediately connected to the president, it will be your ass. Get a move on." He heard the noisy thrust of jet engines in the background.

In what seemed like an eternity, Thomas Kennan was on the line, an edge of irritation in his voice. "Yes, Joe, what is it?"

"We have a major flap developing in the Middle East." The retired one-star general paused, taking a short breath. "Islamic terrorists are cooking up something big—maybe even thermonuclear. I recommend you convene a meeting of your National Security Council today."

"This California event is a big—"

"Mr. President," Campbell interrupted. "Some angry Iranian mullahs have obtained the power to change the world. And now they may be ready to do it."

ONE POINT SIXTEEN MILES AWAY from the White
House, at the Royal Embassy of Saudi Arabia, Prince Khalid bin
Aziz was also on the telephone. The fifty-two-year-old nephew of
King Abdullah, widely known as the Arab Gatsby with his trimmed
goatee and tailored double-breasted suits, was a member of the royal
House of Saud and the Saudi Arabian ambassador to the United
States.

"Was not our arrangement concluded?" Khalid said.

"Disturbing new developments, Your Royal Highness," reported Phillip Gervaise, the CIA chief. "The attorney general's office
is pressing for terrorist trials to be conducted by the Justice Department in federal courts—not by military commissions."

Greeted by silence, Gervaise pressed on. "This means that Muneer Hassan's lawyers will have the right to take depositions from
CIA agents."

"Why should your attorney general's activities be of interest to
me?"

Gervaise broached the subject cautiously. "In open court testimony, it could become common knowledge that al-Qaeda received
financial support from the highest levels of the Saudi government
and that you had advance knowledge of the 9-11 attack but remained
silent."

"Hassan will never talk. His parents are in protective custody in
Riyadh."

"We have a problem," Gervaise explained. "After Hassan was
captured in Afghanistan, he was subjected to enhanced interrogation
techniques by a CIA agent utilizing a short-acting narcotic—a thiopental sodium drip that induced the man to talk. Being one of bin
Laden's top aides, he was able to name three of King Abdullah's
nephews and the chief of Pakistan's air force as his major contacts.
Hassan also reeled off your home and mobile phone numbers, and
described—on videotape—your involvement in channeling funds to
bin Laden before 9-11."

"You were well paid to contain this."

"And I did. The videotape of Hassan's interrogation was never turned over to the 9-11 commission. I claimed the tape was destroyed to protect the safety of undercover operatives—"

Khalid interrupted, "All of the Saudis identified by Hassan are now conveniently dead, and the head of Pakistan's air force, Mushaf Ali Mir, unfortunately died when his plane mysteriously blew up. So, my friend, what is the problem?"

"Until now, the CIA agent involved with Hassan has been silenced by his CIA confidentiality agreement. The man would face a long jail sentence if he were to speak out. However, his confidentiality agreement would be abridged if the agent were required to testify in a federal court."

"Isn't hearsay evidence inadmissible under your rules of evidence?"

Gervaise hesitated. "True." He coughed nervously. "There is a duplicate copy of the Hassan interrogation. The former CIA agent mailed me an excerpted portion of the video with a note explaining this was his life insurance policy."

Khalid said with quiet venom, "Eliminate him."

"The man was a senior black-ops operative who resigned, then disappeared and has fallen off of our radar. It will not be easy, nor inexpensive, to locate him."

"How much will it cost this time to enlist your cooperation?"

"Americans have a saying: 'One hand washes the other.' I have a banking problem, Your Royal Highness. The Justice Department is planning to file court documents to allow the IRS to get information from Swiss banks. Thanks to your largess, I maintain an account at UBS. It would be most appreciated if these funds could be transferred to a friendlier environment, like the Al-Baraka Islamic Bank in Bahrain."

"And we Arabs have a saying: 'One hand full of money is stronger than two hands full of truth.' I will handle your financial problem, Phillip—after the man is dead."

"I've tried to locate him. There is no trace. He's a ghost, not listed as a title-holder to any real estate or vehicle. He has no debts, no liens, no address, no ATM card, and no credit rating. I'll do my best, but right now I'm due at the White House."

"The White House?" Khalid lifted an eyebrow.

In an exasperated tone, Gervaise said, "Our new director of national intelligence is in a panic over an unsubstantiated and probably self-serving admission from a Revolutionary Guard defector. The man claims Iran is preparing a nuclear strike against Israel. Campbell pressured the president into calling the meeting at the White House."

"Do you take this defector's warning seriously?"

"We receive warnings all the time. This isn't the first time we've heard about Islamic terrorists having nuclear weapons. In time, our analysts will sort it all out."

Khalid disconnected the call, a worried look on his face. He mused aloud, "Nothing must interfere with our plan. *Inshallah*— God willing."

TWO POINT SEVEN MILES AWAY from the White House, at Vice President C. J. Landry's residence on the grounds of the United States Naval Observatory, the Reverend Dr. Isaiah Bowman was getting seriously pissed off.

C.J. Landry, the sixty-four-year-old vice president and former senator, was still photogenic, with his coifed mane of wavy silver hair, chiseled features, and eyes that had a calculating shrewdness to them. During his years in the Senate, Landry had earned a reputation as a man with a laser sharp memory and keen intellect. In spite of his cultivated folksy image, Landry had not gained the trust and respect of a man like Thomas Kennan because he was a fool. In fact, he was very smart indeed.

"Isaiah, you got to reconsider running for senator," Landry said to the pastor of the World Church of the Rapture. "If we're gonna beat the Republicans, the party needs Georgia. We think that you're turning off voters with all that Armageddon talk."

Isaiah Bowman stared stonily at the vice president. "Well, how about that," he sniffed. "Did you catch the *Newsweek* article? 'Forty percent of Americans believe the world will end just as the Bible predicts: a battle between Jesus and the antichrist at Armageddon'?"

He waved a fat finger at the vice president. "There are 300,000 Evangelicals in the State of Georgia who believe the literal truth of the Bible's prophecy written by an all-seeing, all-knowing, all-powerful God who chooses to give his people advance warning of cataclysmic events. The end days are coming, C.J. Islam is wicked and evil. Isn't what they do to women evil? Would you like your missus wearing dark clothes, hoods and stuff like that?"

"Isaiah, I've been around long enough to know what wins and what loses elections. Politics is *not* the art of irritating folk. Atheists, agnostics and the uncommitted make up sixteen percent of the population—nearly as many as Baptists. These folk don't congregate, e-mail, or petition like members of organized religions, but they plain don't like mixing religion and politics."

"I am who I am," Bowman interrupted. "Millions watch my television ministry. And I'll tell you what: the Good Book promises that there will be a final showdown in the valley of Armageddon and true believers will find the Rapture. They will be transported to heaven, where, seated next to the right hand of God, they will watch their enemies suffer plagues of boils, sores, locusts and frogs during the several years of retribution that follow."

Landry rose, signaling an end to the meeting. "Sorry, Isaiah, I have to get over to the White House. Kennan asked me to have this friendly chat with you. Don't get me wrong—I think Armageddon has some pluses. I would love to watch a few of my Republican colleagues suffer plagues of any sort through all eternity."

Bowman glowered. "Laugh all you want to, C.J., but tell Thomas Kennan that I'm ahead in the polls and I ain't quittin'. Come November, Georgia is going to elect a pro-life, pro-Second Amendment, conservative minister of God who doesn't believe in pussy-footing when it comes to religion or the Middle East. Despite all his tough talk, this president will never take military action to defend the Jewish state against a nuclear Iran. That's the God's truth and you know it."

The minister also stood up. "And, if you read your Bible, it warns that the same Russian bear that Kennan is trying to cuddle up with will hibernate, then awaken with an evil plan. Ezekiel 38 says Russia will ally with the armies of Islam and come 'like a storm' against Israel.

"We're both ambitious country boys," Isaiah Bowman added with a thin smile and a wink. "We understand each other. Not as your minister, but as your friend, I'm telling you Armageddon's coming soon, and Israel is going to be the focal point. You best stay ahead of the curve."

Landry wasn't listening. His mind was already mulling on the urgent meeting of the National Security Council called by the president.

...5

IN THE SECOND SUB-BASEMENT LEVEL beneath the White House, Joseph Campbell, the director of national intelligence, sat in the Situation Room, steeling himself for a difficult meeting ahead. He fidgeted with control buttons for the room's six large monitors. Each monitor was equipped with split-screen technology and secure, advanced communications equipment, enabling President Kennan to maintain command of U.S. forces scattered around the globe.

The former general gazed at the cream-colored grass cloth wallpaper, reflecting on when he was a cadet at West Point in 1962: Kennedy's Security Council had met in this very room during the Cuban missile crisis. *We could be on the brink again*, he mused.

Congress had created Campbell's position of "intelligence czar" after 9-11 to force coordination between the hidebound American intelligence bureaucracies. Appointed a few months back by President Kennan, Campbell was quick to learn that his high-sounding position commanded little actual power over the fifty-billion dollar annual budget—the major portion of which was spent on spy satellites and high-tech listening devices under Pentagon control.

I'm a fucking eunuch in this job, he thought. Campbell had also discovered that he had minimal responsibility for hiring and firing decisions in the sprawling intelligence infrastructure. He was annoyed but not deterred. He had never failed to give one hundred percent effort to any assignment, either on the athletic fields of West Point or the killing fields of Viet Nam. Campbell wasn't about to stop now, especially where his best friend Tom Kennan was concerned.

Their relationship stretched back forty years to the U.S. Military Academy, where Kennan and Campbell were roommates. All-American running back "Injun-Joe" Campbell was favorably compared by sports writers to another Native American: football legend Jim Thorpe. His roommate, First Captain Thomas Kennan, graduated as class valedictorian. Lieutenant Thomas Kennan spent the summer after graduation at the Army Airborne School at Fort Benning, Georgia, before being accepted for a Rhodes scholarship and completing his degree at Magdalen College at the University of Oxford in August 1968.

After leaving England, Kennan joined the 1st Infantry Division in Vietnam as a staff officer in operations, earning high commendations. A year later, he requested and received command of a rifle company. One month into his command, Kennan was shot four times by a Viet Cong soldier with an AK-47. The wounded Kennan shouted orders to his men, who counterattacked and defeated the Viet Cong force. He was awarded the Silver Star for his actions during the encounter.

Campbell thought about the different paths he and his roommate had followed. After graduation, Joe Campbell had volunteered for the Studies and Observations Group, a cover title for the Vietnam War's covert special warfare group. They mined roads, rescued downed pilots and vectored artillery and air strikes against enemy troop concentrations.

His Viet Nam reverie was disturbed by the arrival of national security staff members grumbling as they handed over their electronic mobile devices to Secret Service agents. Campbell turned and scanned the faces of the people entering the room.

Cassia Politto, the secretary of state, nodded gloomily to Campbell and settled into one of the steel-blue leather upholstered seats around the long cherry wood conference table. He respected Cassia Politto; he knew she was the first female and first Hispanic to be president of Yale University. He had heard that before that, Politto had headed a school of advanced international studies, a division of

Johns Hopkins University based in Washington, D.C. Campbell guessed the tall woman intentionally masked her natural good looks. She wore no rings on her fingers, no makeup on her attractive face. She held back a troublesome forelock with her left hand as she shook hands firmly with the chairman of the Joint Chiefs, Admiral Jeb Baysinger.

Baysinger gave Campbell a mock salute. The admiral was a distinguished-looking man with an aquiline face and regal blue eyes. He was dressed in his service dress blue uniform, including a twenty-ribbon bar under the gold insignia of a submarine flanked by two dolphins. Baysinger and Campbell had competed in the 1963 Army-Navy game in Philadelphia. Navy won 21-15. Jeb Baysinger never failed to tease Campbell about Navy's victory when they met. Campbell trusted the man.

Secretary of Defense Sanfred Fishman, a stocky, big-boned man in his fifties, entered the Situation Room, studiously ignored Campbell, and took a seat. Fishman was dressed as usual in a tailored wool suit and silk tie; his substantial belly poked through the front of his unbuttoned suit jacket. Campbell gazed stonily back at the former Wall Street banker who had become CEO of General Aerospace Corporation before being tapped by Kennan to streamline the defense department. Campbell considered Fishman a beefy, sweating political backslapper.

The director of the CIA was the last to arrive. Phillip Gervaise slipped quietly into a chair at the far end. Campbell nodded, thinking, *You prize asshole, you really believe gathering intelligence is about committee meetings, electronic eavesdropping and computer printouts—not field operatives.* Conversation in the room was muted. No one wanted to be bantering about the Redskins or the World Series when the president arrived.

PRECISELY AT TWELVE NOON, the room hushed as Thomas Kennan entered, along with Vice President C. J. Landry.

Everyone stood. The president smiled. "The media portrays you as my military junta, so it's appropriate to say, *at ease*."

There was polite laughter. The participants evidenced cautious apprehension and professional unease. Being summoned on a weekend had everyone on edge.

Kennan's geniality slowly dropped away. His mouth tightened. "Joseph, you threatened the head of my Secret Service detail; now suppose you fill *me* in."

Campbell faced the president. He began in an uneasy tone. "Sir. During the last forty-eight hours we have received some disturbing developments. NSA reports levels of 'chatter' on a scale comparable to the run-up to 9-11. And the CIA has received a stream of warnings from friendly intelligence agencies—"

"What kind of chatter?"

"Much of it in code, sir. NSA is still having problems getting good linguists—"

Kennan broke in. "Well then, what kind of warnings?"

"Alerts of an attack against Israeli interests involving an as yet unknown number of nuclear weapons in the ten to twenty kiloton range."

"On what evidence do you base this doomsday scenario?"

"The warnings come from friendly intelligence services: Germany, Pakistan and Jordan. It was our embassy in Pakistan before 9-11 that alerted the State Department of bin Ladin's plan for a major attack on American soil. The warnings were ignored. Our ambassador in Islamabad has received information directly from the Pakistani spy agency, the Inter-Services Intelligence directorate. Rumors are circulating of a major event being planned against Israel."

"Rumors aren't much to act on, Joseph," Vice President Landry said.

Campbell wiped his sweaty forehead. "Eight days before the September 11th attack, the head of Jordan's General Intelligence Department informed our CIA station chief in Amman that 'credible sources' advised him the al Qaeda network was planning an attack on the United States homeland using aircraft. Like the Pakistani warnings, the Jordanian's were also ignored.

"Yesterday, Director Gervaise supplied me with a communication from the same Jordanian GID reporting that an unidentified Middle Eastern-based group was in the advanced stages of a significant operation against Israeli targets."

Campbell added, "We also heard from Germany's Federal Intelligence Service: shipments of Russian-cloned, Chinese or North Korean-produced missiles are being delivered to Iran."

Kennan turned to the head of the CIA. "Do you share Joseph's views, Phillip?"

"Not entirely, sir," Gervaise hedged. "In defense of the Agency, prior to 9-11, there was a hiring freeze and a lot of experienced personnel retired. The shortage of money and people seriously impacted the Agency's analysis capabilities—"

"That's not entirely true, Phillip," interrupted the vice president. "I agree that after the end of the Cold War, the CIA's functions were underfunded, but that's not why things went wrong," C.J. Landry drawled. "They went wrong because we had a totally dysfunctional, politicized organization handling our intelligence matters. Hopefully, that's been corrected."

Phillip Gervaise flushed. "Every day our agency is inundated with reports of suspected terrorist acts around the world." He paused for effect. "Israel, Jordan, Afghanistan and Pakistan want to keep their foreign aid rolling in; their intelligence services pass on rumors of real or imaginary terrorist threats in order to sustain our goodwill—"

Campbell cut in. "Tell them about Zakariya."

All eyes turned back to Gervaise.

"Yesterday, our London station debriefed a double-agent, a former member of the Iranian Revolutionary Guard. The man claimed, I repeat *claimed*, to have personal knowledge that Iran is preparing to launch nuclear warhead missiles at Israeli targets. The delivery systems are reported to be Chinese-made M-9 and M-11 short-range ballistic missiles. Zakariya is the Iranian's name. He is being flown to Langley for in-depth lie-detector screening and psychological evaluation."

The president's features stiffened. The war room was silent. The only sound was the soft humming of the air conditioning system. Kennan ran his hand through his hair, thinking, his agile mind dissecting the important from the trivial. "I don't want reports quoting some unhappy Iranian scientist or guesses from analysts. I want absolute, incontrovertible proof Iran is plotting a nuclear strike aimed at Israel." As an afterthought, he asked, "Did the Iranian specify targets or the timing of the alleged attack?"

"One target was Tel Aviv, the economic center; another, the Negev Nuclear Research Center in Dimona. And the third was Megiddo in the Jezreel Valley. For psychological reasons, an attack at Megiddo would resonate through the Middle East, asserting Iran's claim to leadership of the Islamic world."

"Magiddo is just a pile of rocks," Defense Secretary Fishman blurted out.

"Yes, Sandy, Megiddo is just a pile of rocks," Gervaise echoed. "Magiddo is also the biblical site known by its Greek name—*Armageddon.*"

Vice President Landry jerked forward in his chair.

Kennan frowned. "We spend fifty billion a year on our intelligence efforts, with your CIA getting a lion's share, Phillip. Can't you or the wizards at NSA with their super secret global eavesdropping technology confirm that Iran is getting missiles from China or North Korea?"

Before Gervaise could respond, Cassia Politto spoke up. "Mr. President, I don't believe China is involved. They are the major importer of Saudi crude and are also betting big in Iraq and Iran. Beijing is filling the void left by Western firms. They have signed contracts for eight billion in oil and gas deals with Tehran. Today China is Iran's biggest trading partner. They would stand to lose too much by abetting a Middle Eastern catastrophe that could impact their energy sources."

Sandy Fishman quipped, "We invest over a billion dollars in Iraq, and the damn Chinese reap the benefits."

The CIA director cleared his throat. "As to timing, our informant reported that the attack would occur on a Muslim holiday— the day on which Abraham was believed to be willing to sacrifice his son. Presuming the man's information is true, the Day of Sacrifice falls on November 5th. That's six days from now."

The silence that followed was haunting.

Finally, Kennan said tersely, "If the Iranians are able—and, God forbid, willing—to equip high-speed ballistic missiles with nuclear warheads, they would be in position to accomplish in six minutes what it took Adolf Hitler six years to do—kill more than six million Jews."

KENNAN LEANED BACK IN HIS CHAIR, closed his eyes and massaged his neck muscles. Turning to the chairman of the Joint Chiefs, he said, "Jeb, you commanded an atomic submarine. What is the damage assessment of a 20-kiloton bomb?"

"Mr. President," Baysinger began, "if I might point out, Israel occupies a land mass three hundred miles long and one hundred and fifty miles wide. However, ninety percent of the population is clustered around Jerusalem and Tel Aviv. A nuclear strike on Tel Aviv would not only kill a significant percentage of the population, but would also wipe out Israel's industrial infrastructure. The radioactive fallout would render the landscape uninhabitable and might make the area for 100 miles downwind uninhabitable for weeks or years—"

Kennan interrupted. "I'm confused. If memory serves, two of the targets are Megiddo and Tel Aviv. Jerusalem is 35 miles away, to say nothing of the crowded West Bank Muslim communities. These bombs would kill both Arabs and Jews."

Fishman said, "Apparently Muslim radicals believe Allah can do anything, even produce a bomb with radiation that only kills Jews and produces no fallout."

Kennan shot the defense secretary a hard look.

Baysinger continued, "The bomb we dropped on Japan was an enriched uranium gun-type device of 12 kilotons. If the Iranians used 20 kiloton bombs, the results in each of the target areas will be exponentially greater than Hiroshima."

The sounds of exhaled breaths could be heard around the room.

"What's Israel's position, Joseph?"

Campbell shrugged and shook his head.

Kennan looked annoyed. He picked up the receiver of a black telephone and pressed a single button. A White House operator came on the line. "Yes, Mr. President?"

"Get me Israel's Prime Minister Ephraim Chpindel on a secure line."

After a few minutes, the White House operator said, "You are connected, sir."

"Mr. Prime Minister, this is Thomas Kennan."

"Mr. President," a weary voice replied. "What can I do for you?"

Kennan inhaled. "Our intelligence services report unsubstantiated, but credibly-sourced information concerning a possible Iranian nuclear missile strike against Israel—within days."

Ephraim Chpindel did not respond.

Kennan continued, "Naturally, we are concerned about your people's safety and a potential blow-up in the Middle East. How seriously do you assess the threat?"

"Mr. President," Chpindel said, a slight edge to his voice. "The Jewish people are continually threatened by enemies, as we have been for thousands of years. If we are certain in advance of any serious threat to our citizens, we will initiate the necessary remedial actions."

"Ephraim, I respect your right to protect yourself, but I urge caution before considering a preemptive attack."

"Thomas," Chpindel said quietly. "If you had known in advance the identity and location of the plotters of your 9-11 disaster that killed 2700 civilians in New York and 184 at the Pentagon, and who were also trying to attack the White House—would you have taken pre-emptive actions?"

Kennan was silent.

"Mr. President, it is six a.m. here in Tel Aviv. I apologize if my remarks are insensitive. I was sleeping. I will look into the situation. Give my regards to your lovely wife. Goodbye, sir."

KENNAN GRIMACED. He looked around the Situation Room. "They should rename this the Ulcer Center. Anyone have a recommendation?"

Gervaise raised a hand. "If Israel is not on full alert and not requesting help from us, maybe we should do nothing. Israel might be less intractable about West Bank settlements if something happens and they bleed a little."

The vice president coughed. "I was a young congressman in 1973 at the time of the Yom Kippur War." His syrupy accent faded notably. "Kissinger tried to delay a much-needed airlift of weapons to Israel, even as Israelis were dying by the hundreds repelling the surprise attacks from Egypt and Syria."

Landry looked over his glasses at the CIA director. "Kissinger's strategy was much like yours, Phillip. In order to force Israel to be more accommodating to our Mideast peace plans, he proposed letting the Arabs win some territory and some self respect, thereby setting up the possibility of serious land-for-peace bargaining."

He looked around the room. "Kissinger's plan backfired, and Nixon ordered the airlift to go full-steam ahead." He winked at Cassia Politto. "If the secretary of state will excuse my language, Nixon and Kissinger nearly shit themselves when Israel announced they were preparing to deploy nuclear weapons against their Arab enemies." He paused. "And also against Russia itself, who was supplying arms and advisors."

"Were they bluffing?" Kennan asked.

"Not one bit. Our intelligence community confirmed Israel's claim using our KH-11 spy planes. Israeli missile launchers had been hidden in the side of a hill at Hirbat Zachariah. The launchers were in the open, deliberately, I guess, for American and Russian photo interpreters to spot them. The photos included hollowed-out nuclear storage bunkers and huge blast doors with railroad tracks leading to a nearby missile launch site." He chortled. "On that occasion, our government had no problem locating weapons of mass destruction."

Landry paused. "It was Israel's Samson Option."

"Samson Option?" Cassia Politto asked, raising her eyebrows.

"A term used to describe Israel's strategy of massive retaliation with nuclear weapons as a last resort against nations who threaten its existence. If you'll remember your Bible, the Philistines captured Samson, his eyes were torn out, and he was put on display for public entertainment in some temple in Gaza.

"Samson asked God to give him back his strength, and he cried out, 'Let my soul die with the Philistines.' With that he pushed apart the temple pillars, bringing down the roof and killing himself and his enemies. For Israel, the Samson Option is their way of saying, 'Never again.' "

The president looked at Secretary of Defense Sanfred Fishman. "Sandy, does the Pentagon have updates on Israel's current nuclear capability?"

Fishman's total recall was legendary. He said, "Israel has between 75 and 200 thermonuclear weapons, each in the multiple-megaton range, plus as many as 400 nuclear weapons that could be launched from land, sea and air. This gives them a second strike option even if much of their country is destroyed."

Thomas Kennan sat like a tensed spring. "You were right insisting on this meeting, Joseph. Israel is the fuse of Armageddon—a fuse that could ignite at any time. We don't have many options, and we don't have much time."

"We have increased satellite reconnaissance over Israel and Iran," Gervaise said.

"Sir," Campbell volunteered. "All the satellite reconnaissance in the world isn't the same as agents on the ground to know what is really going on."

Kennan looked hard at Gervaise. "What assets do we have in Iran and Israel?"

Gervaise felt a knot in his gut. "It takes time—"

"Obviously, we haven't got time," Kennan interrupted.

The CIA director squirmed in his seat. "The uncomfortable truth is that field operatives in the Agency's clandestine division have an average of five years' experience. Not five years in the field, but five years total time in. The dearth of experience is so bad that we've re-hired former CIA case officers in their 60s and 70s to come back, on contract, to help out."

Kennan listened, but was silent.

"With your approval, sir," Gervaise continued, "I will immediately initiate reactivation of seasoned operatives with Middle East experience. Unfortunately, they're spread around the country. We could use help in locating them."

For the first time since the meeting began, Thomas Kennan allowed a smile. "With NSA's 20,000 employees at Fort Meade, and the zillion dollar P415 surveillance program, they ought to help you do the job."

Thank you, Jesus, Phillip Gervaise thought.

Kennan stood up, glanced anxiously at his watch, and prepared to leave. "Regrettably, money is the mother's milk of politics. If we all want to keep our jobs come the next election, I cannot ignore wealthy Hollywood contributors. I'll fly back tonight. Nothing discussed in this room goes out beyond this circle unless approved by me personally. No pillow talk; no staff talk. Even rumors could create hysteria worldwide—confusion that we don't need. All of you are to remain in D.C. on standby."

He turned to Campbell. "Joe, why don't you go over to the Hill today and see the chairman of the House and Senate committees? I don't want to blindside them on this. In addition to Israelis being in harm's way, there could be thousands of Americans in the area." His eyes hardened. "And if there really is an Iranian threat, I want confirmation. And I want it yesterday!"

...6

THE CIA DIRECTOR CRADLED HIS CELL PHONE as he sped along the winding tree-lined George Washington Parkway. A light November wind worried the multicolored leaves. "Get Schreck," he barked to his secretary. "My office, three o'clock."

Exiting at McLean, Gervaise entered Langley's south gate, identified himself at the speaker box, nodded absently to the guard, and parked in his reserved space. He hustled up the short flight of stairs to the entrance of the CIA's Headquarters Building, under the suspended scale models of the U-2, A-12, and D-21 photoreconnaissance aircraft in the atrium.

Gervaise paused in one of the building's curved tunnels containing a copper grid shield to protect conversations from outside listening devices. Looking around, the CIA chief punched in a programmed phone number. "Your Royal Highness, everything is under control." Click.

"WHAT'S THE CRISIS?" Dorothy Schreck asked.

"Ours is not to reason why," Gervaise chuckled. "We're like the local constabulary. Nobody likes us and nobody wants to give us a decent salary, but when there's trouble, who do they run crying to for help?" His eyes glistened. "You should have heard me bullshit Kennan about being short-handed. He authorized me to activate experienced agents. I want a list of our top retired operatives. ASAP." He tented his fingers on his desk. "A few come to mind, one in particular: Avram Markus, the former Mossad operative who had connections with the Russians. If he is still alive, we need to locate him."

Schreck looked up sharply. "You're going to reactivate the Scorpion?"

"The president authorized me to use all government assets. I want you to connect with NSA at Ft. Meade and Echelon's P415 surveillance programs Silkworth and Sire. If they give you static, tell them to call the White House. I want round-the-clock phone tracing on Markus, plus e-mails, bank transfers, credit card transactions, home mortgages, investment accounts, travel and telephone records." He added more categories. "Also check the IRS, departments of motor vehicles, and find out where his Social Security and pension checks are sent to." He smiled. "If the old fart is still breathing, we'll find him."

Schreck narrowed her eyes. "That's your plan A to abort an Iranian attack?"

ONE HOUR LATER, Schreck was sitting at her desk scanning computer printouts forwarded from NSA cryptologists. Her phone rang. She noted the information, thanked the caller and hung up. A veteran named Avram Markus had been fitted for Phonak hearing aids at the VA Medical Center in West Palm Beach, Florida in April of the previous year. "At least you're still alive," she muttered to herself.

Two black coffees later, Schreck uncovered a strong lead. Markus' pension checks were being forwarded to an attorney in Baltimore. She called in Gervaise to listen in to her conversation.

"Mr. Breger," she said on the speakerphone. "My name is Dorothy Schreck. I'm the assistant director of central intelligence—"

"Is this some joke?" Breger interrupted.

"If you like, I can give you the CIA's number. Call me at my office in Langley."

Breger's tone softened. "What is it you want?"

"You have a client by the name of Avram Markus?"

There was no response.

"We are trying to contact Mr. Markus relative to a very important matter."

"Miss...."

"Schreck," she said.

"Miss Schreck, I'm certain you are aware the attorney-client privilege is a legal concept that protects communications between a client and his lawyer and insures those communications are confidential. I'm afraid that I can be of no service to—"

Gervaise broke in on the speakerphone. "Breger, this is CIA Director Phillip Gervaise. I am sure *you* are aware that under the USA Patriot Act, anyone obstructing an investigation affecting national security can be arrested, jailed, named as an unindicted co-conspirator, and receive a sentence of up to five years."

He glanced at the wall clock and winked at Schreck. "It is now 4:15 pm. If I don't get Markus' address in less than a minute, I will contact our Baltimore office. You will be marched out of your building in handcuffs within the hour."

"I was just trying to protect—"

A hoarse laugh. "What's it going to be, Breger? Your conscience or your career?"

"Hold on a minute," the lawyer mumbled.

Schreck whispered to Gervaise, "We don't have a Baltimore office."

He turned off the speakerphone for a moment. "Lying is a necessary skill in our line of work—as you well know."

Breger came back on the phone, breathing heavily. "I forward Social Security and pension checks to the following post office box number in Fort Pierce, Florida."

"Your nation thanks you for your service," Gervaise said, jotting down the number and hanging up. He turned to Schreck. "Contact the postmaster general if you have to. Get me an address for this P.O. box number."

Twenty minutes later Dorothy Schreck called Gervaise with the information.

The CIA chief left his office, pausing again under the copper grid shield. Looking around to insure he was alone, Gervaise punched in a private number.

The phone was picked up. No one answered.

"Eagle waste disposal?"

"Yeh?" a deep voice answered.

"I have a pickup."

...7

A LARGE-BONED, SLOVENLY-DRESSED LADY carrying two shopping bags sauntered slowly up Wisconsin Avenue in Georgetown. She paused to look in the window of a retail store featuring handmade French and Italian ceramics, linens and other decorative home accessories. With effort, Dorothy Schreck lugged her bags up three brick steps and entered the shop. She caught the eye of the owner, who motioned with his head and eyes—upstairs.

In the small private office, Schreck greeted Joseph Campbell. He gave her a nod, then closed and locked the door.

The assistant director of the Agency sat down heavily. "Those stairs are a bitch."

"I've got a hell of a lot on my plate," Campbell grumped. "What's so damned important that we have to meet like spies in a cramped office over a gift shop?"

"Joseph," she gasped, still wheezing heavily. "Face it—we *are* spies. But you are one of the few spooks in this town I trust. Hemingway said, 'The most essential gift for a good writer is a built-in, shock-proof shit detector.' Maybe I should have been a writer, because I'm detecting a lot of shit coming from my boss. He came back from your meeting saying that you were in a panic over the Iranian missile threat—"

Campbell broke in angrily, "He was ordered not to— Never mind. Go on."

"The first thing Phillip did was to initiate a manhunt for one retired agent."

"Phillip isn't one of my admirers, and I assure you, it's mutual, but if your boss can enlist competent field agents to help us resolve a serious situation, I'm all in favor."

36

Schreck shrugged. "This particular agent retired after a falling-out with Gervaise. Rumor has it there was bad blood between the two of them. Something happened. Very hush hush. Markus fell off the radar. He disappeared and became a ghost."

She took a deep breath. "I know I'm violating a dozen oaths by mentioning this. Avram Markus had a videotape that was intentionally destroyed by Phillip Gervaise and not turned over to the 9-11 commission."

Campbell's eyes widened.

"I think Gervaise is using the presidential authority for a personal vendetta."

"You know that I can't get in the middle of an Agency personnel situation."

Dorothy Schreck put her hand on Joe Campbell's wrist and squeezed gently. "Trust me on this one. Markus worked with the Mossad before he joined the CIA. We worked together. He was the best of the best in the Agency. Avram might actually be able to be of help to you. His code name was the Scorpion."

"The Scorpion?"

"As a kid, Markus was hiking with friends southwest of Jerusalem, near Beersheba. He tripped into a large nest of *Leiurus quinquestriatus.*"

"Of what?"

Schreck laughed. "That's Latin for the world's deadliest arachnid—the Israeli desert scorpion. He was rushed to the closest hospital, near death. They pumped him full of anti-toxin; somehow the kid survived and became immune to the bite of a scorpion. He collected desert scorpions and milked them for their deadly venom. Code-named the Scorpion, Markus became the Agency's most effective... counter-weapon."

Campbell rose, shaking his head. "Sorry. I can't waste time on one old assassin."

She hesitated before speaking. "This is very personal, Joseph. I'm a big woman. Men never found me attractive. I didn't have a positive self-image. That's why I threw myself into my work. Avram made me feel that I was beautiful as well as a competent intelligence officer. It wasn't sexual." She took a deep breath. "He changed my life."

Campbell glanced at his watch impatiently. "All right," he said warily. "If you can find this guy and if your boss doesn't object, introduce me to Spiderman."

...8

Guardian.co.uk home

Double Shooting in Mayfair District

London, November 3ʳᵈ—A post-mortem examination is being carried out for two victims shot dead in a Mayfair hotel by an unknown assailant. One was a fifty-year-old man identified as an Iranian citizen, Herro Zakariya. The second victim was a seventy-year-old night desk clerk, Maime Carlson. Police responding to an anonymous telephone tip discovered the bodies.

Detective Chief Inspector John Mackenzie said, "Shooting incidents are still rather rare in London. Ms. Carlson was struck twice in the chest, and she could not be saved. Ms. Carlson's family was very distraught, as you would expect. It is a traumatic, violent way for a loved one to go." He added, "The Iranian was shot once in the head and twice in the chest. A message was scrawled in blood on the wall: 'Death to American spies.' "

Radisson Edwardian Sussex Hotel employees say Mr. Zakariya was seen in the company of American embassy officials, who picked him up in the morning and delivered him at dinnertime yesterday.

Detective Chief Inspector John Mackenzie added, "We are working with the community, asking if anyone observed anything suspicious in the vicinity of Gloucester Street during the early morning hours last night."

Flowers, including three bunches of white roses, have been laid at the foot of the police cordon taping off the scene at Radisson Edwardian Sussex Hotel. American Embassy officials have refused comment.

"WHAT DO YOU MEAN, 'ZAKARIYA'S DEAD'?" Gervaise barked. "Christ, Howard, I ordered you to babysit him until the flight."

"I fucked up, Phil. What else can I say? We had minders on him until midnight. When my men left, the door was double-locked and chained. They were scheduled to return to the hotel at 6 a.m. Whoever did him was a pro. I'm really sorry."

"Oh, the president will love to hear this," Gervaise groaned, hanging up and checking his watch. *Almost eleven*, he mused, excited in spite of Roland Howard's call. With ten million safely stored in Bahrain, it was time to consider retirement to St. Barts in the Caribbean.

He heard a soft knock at the door. He thought it strange he had heard no car sounds, no footsteps and no barking from Colby, his powerful Rottweiler watchdog. Gervaise patted his shoulder holster, looked through the peephole, and smiled as he unlatched and unlocked the door.

"What a pleasant surprise," he said. "Come in. To what do I owe this honor?"

"Dorothy Schreck sent me over with a package, sir."

The Rottweiler growled. "Down, Colby," Gervaise commanded. "Sit, boy. Stay."

A'isha Khouri stepped inside as Gervaise closed the door. As the CIA director turned, he stared into the muzzle of a Beretta 9 mm silencer. Four short pops were heard. One into Gervaise's head, one into the watchdog's brain, and two into the CIA chief's heart as he stumbled backward, one hand groping his ruined chest and the other reaching for his gun before his knees buckled under him and he crumpled dead to the floor.

Outside, Alie tugged up her coat collar again. The temperature hovered at forty-five degrees, unseasonably cool for November in Washington.

...9

ON THE DAY HIS DESTINY RETURNED TO CLAIM HIM, Avram Markus looked into the bathroom mirror when he went to pee at 4 a.m. His face showed the years: every crease. He still had a full head of hair, all white now. He saw reflected the heavy-lidded blue eyes and bushy eyebrows. It was a common-looking face, one that had served him well in his chameleon years. In Europe, Avram had passed easily for a Frenchman or German or Russian, because he spoke the languages fluently.

Avram Markus wondered if anything had been resolved by escaping to Florida to spend the rest of his life under a hot sun near the ocean, always looking over his shoulder. He had tried to disappear once before in his life and knew the truth—geography solved nothing. He had lived a life of secrets and lies so long, he knew no other way.

Avram slept fitfully for an hour until the prickling fear of an unknown presence awakened him. The luminous dial on his watch read 5 a.m. He heard footsteps as the old wooden floorboards in the living room creaked. *Two men, or maybe three*, he thought. He felt an adrenaline surge, but remained still, betraying nothing. With deliberate slowness he reached for his Walther P99 pistol stored in the night table.

A flashlight beam splayed across Markus' face, blinding him for a second. "No heroics," the deep voice said. "No disrespect, but you're out of your depth, old man."

The bed lamp was switched on, flooding the room with a muted amber light. Peering through crusted eyelids, Markus saw two men and recognized their type immediately: tight jaws, fixed expressions and alert postures. Their bodies were stocky but toned. *Gervaise's*

42

subcontractors, ex-SEALs or Delta Force, he thought. One was big and dark, the other more leanly muscled. The larger of the two said, "You were at Gitmo, right? You know the drill. Tell us where the videotape is."

Markus felt a vein throbbing in his forehead. Years before he would have remained impassive in dangerous situations, but now his heart thudded. He knew instinctively that these men in his bedroom were killers.

"Let me put on a robe. My hearing aid is in the living room," Avram grumbled.

Both men trailed him into the sparse living room, their Glock 23's held loosely in hand. The walls were bare, with faint outlines where framed paintings had once hung. The books were the only personal items: no photographs of family or friends, no stack of mail. A cracked black leather sofa and a wicker chair were grouped around a glass coffee table with an oversized planter positioned in the center.

"The tape, Pops," the leader repeated, "or we go the hard route."

Markus scratched his head. "I think I hid them in that planter on the coffee table."

The big man nodded and plunged his left hand into the planter. "Jesus," he screamed, wrenching his hand out. Three giant, hairy black scorpions were attached to the gunman's wrist. In a panic, he shook his arm wildly to dislodge the scorpions. Agitated, the arachnids flipped their tails over their bodies and stung.

"They fuckin' bit me," he shrieked, dropping his gun and trying to shake them off. The physical exertions sped the venom coursing through his bloodstream, causing paralysis. The man clutched at his throat and fell to the floor in a coma.

His partner was momentarily distracted. Markus smashed his right knee into the gunman's midsection. At the same time, he spun him around, cupped the base of the man's neck with both hands, and with a clean jerk pulled sharply back. He heard the neck break with an audible snap. He held the limp man a few seconds, then let him drop.

Markus retrieved his Walther P99 from the bedroom, attached the silencer, and stood over the large man in a coma. From engrained habit, he employed the basic Mozambique technique: two in the heart and one in the head. Then he opened the front door. A dark Toyota sedan was parked across the street, a driver behind the wheel. He walked over to the startled man and pointed the gun. "Please join your companions."

Once inside, Markus calmly repeated the drill. The silencer dulled the sound of the shots. Markus took a deep breath and slowly lugged each of the three heavy dead bodies out behind the house. He buried the killers in the soft sandy soil, got a mop and cleaned up the living room.

In the driver's pocket, he found the car keys, put on gloves, and drove the Toyota four blocks over to Avenue D, parking the car in front of a rundown bar. He knew the vehicle was toxic; Gervaise's people would be wildly issuing all-points bulletins. Avram left the keys in the ignition and walked home.

Back in the kitchen, he picked up a bag containing live crickets, which he dumped into the planter, whistling softly. Three large scorpions scurried across the floor, attaching themselves to his hand; one at a time he gently placed them into the container with the others.

Markus fixed a cup of coffee and watched impassively as the dozen arachnids inside the planter stung, crushed and chewed the crickets into a semi-liquid state, then sucked up the remains with their tiny mouths.

...10

AT 8 A.M., DOROTHY SCHRECK'S PHONE JANGLED.

"Sorry to break it to you this way," Joseph Campbell said in a grave voice. "Director Phillip Gervaise was murdered sometime during the night."

"Phillip... murdered?"

"The Metropolitan police are handling the situation. I've spoken to the president. He agrees you should take over as temporary director of the Agency. Congressional confirmation is not automatic; we'll worry about that later. Be in my office at 3 p.m. By the way, congratulations." Click.

Schreck gulped her black coffee while firing up her computer. On a legal pad she wrote down the Fort Pierce address she had given Gervaise. Keying in another screen, she found the phone number she was seeking, dialed it, delivered her message, and hung up. Her phone rang again.

"What the hell's going on?" Roland Howard snapped over the secure hookup from the London Embassy. "First Zakariya gets whacked, now Gervaise. You the big kahuna now?"

"News travels fast. You have a problem with that, Roland?"

"I have a problem believing these two murders were coincidental. That's what I have a problem with. There was a laptop found in the room with Herro Zakariya's body. The Metropolitan police didn't spill it to the press. They took one look at Herro's computer and passed it on to MI-6; it contains Iranian missile plans and blueprints. As a courtesy, Sir Peter Heller briefed me on what they downloaded so far."

"And?"

"Among the many documents on the laptop, investigators found drawings with modifications to Iran's ballistic missiles to accommodate nuclear warheads. Also, they found photos showing the launch site of a Chinese M-10 rocket that Iran tested in September at a previously unknown missile location 230 kilometers southeast of Tehran. MI-6 is certain that Iran can deliver nuclear payloads, but they don't believe they have nuclear warheads yet."

Schreck placed a finger thoughtfully against her lips. She remained silent.

"There's more good news," Howard continued. "It looks like the Iranians are following the same path as North Korea—that is, in addition to short-range missiles, they are also developing a long-range missile technology. Peter Heller showed me a photograph of a building about 40 meters in length, which MI-6 says is similar in size to the Taepodong long-range missile assembly facility in North Korea."

"Long-range meaning—intercontinental?"

"It raises two interesting possibilities: one, that internal opponents of the Iranian leadership could have forged the documents to implicate the government; or two, that the documents were planted by Tehran itself as a warning to the West not to try and interfere in Iran as we did in Iraq."

"What's your opinion?"

Roland Howard was a seasoned CIA operative with fifteen years' experience in the Middle East. He wasn't going to allow himself to be pressured. Schreck heard him inhale audibly. "We screwed up the 9-11 warnings. It taught me a hard lesson: quick response to timely intelligence rules the day. There is always a chance this could be a scam, but Christ, Zakariya's laptop contained so many documents proving missile delivery capabilities that it would be irresponsible not to take this seriously.

"Since you asked for my opinion, I think the towel heads are gearing up for something nasty. I've been in the Agency a long time —too long maybe. I'm forced to accept that religious fanatics play by their own misguided rules. All that remains is for these crazy Iranian mullahs to get their hands on a few nuclear warheads to load on their missiles, and then the genie is out of the fucking bottle."

...11

THE SUN PINKED THE SKYLINE, and the old man looked at his watch, knowing time was short. He expected Gervaise to react quickly, this time with experienced black-ops teams dispatched to his home.

One by one Markus lifted out his scorpions, enclosing them in a homemade milking device that encased the scorpion's jutting tail, preventing it from using its padipalps to pinch or sting. He plugged in a small electric apparatus. The arachnids were each given a series of low voltage shocks, causing them to eject venom into a collecting vial. Markus filled three vials, then reached down into the scorpion-filled planter and removed two large freezer bags. He spilled out the contents on the table: credit cards under different names with driver's licenses to match; money in various currencies; and CIA-issued passports that he'd kept after jobs were done, claiming they had been lost along the way. One was British, one Canadian, both of good quality. He examined them carefully, checking the laminated photographs.

In the second sealed plastic bag was a box of videocassette tapes. He toted the planter into the back yard, tilting it to enable the scorpions to crawl away into the sandy dune over the three un-marked graves. Avram took the videos, his Walther P99 handgun, and the vials of scorpion venom. He packed an electronic gadget, clothes, pills, hearing aids, batteries, and a bent wire hanger into a knapsack, grabbed his cane, and walked out into the brightening early morning sunshine. Avram Markus knew one thing for certain. He was not going to run. He was through running.

A warm wind was blowing off the Indian River, the tempera-ture already pushing into the seventies. The city marina was bustling. Charter boat captains chatted each other up on cell phones. A swarm of early risers pressed forward, eager to board the fishing boats readying to cast off from the Ft. Pierce inlet into the Atlantic.

Avram sat quietly on a bench at Marina Square, observing people parking and unloading fishing gear, attentive to the ones boarding all-day charters. He sniffed the saline odor of the ocean mixed with the acrid smell of marine diesel fuel.

As the last boats cast off, heading out the inlet toward the sea, he searched for an older model car parked by one of the all-day charter customers. Nobody gave the gentle-looking old man with the soft smile a second look as he leaned his cane against a 1999 Isuzu wagon, unzipped his knapsack, and unraveled the wire hanger until it was straight. He formed a small hook at the end and snagged the door lock open.

Avram checked that the car was in neutral, the parking brake on, then took from his bag a screwdriver, wire stripper, and insulated gloves. He opened the hood, located a red coil wire on the left side of the engine, and ran a wire from the battery to the coil.

The old CIA operative planned to drive north on US 1 to the long term parking area at Melbourne International Airport. There he would ditch the Isuzu and pick up a Greyhound bus at the airport terminal to Jacksonville and from there to Washington to settle with Gervaise. He had credit cards, but didn't want to use them. Best to work with cash.

Bending over gave him an ache in his lower back. With effort he pushed the flat blade screwdriver between the wheel and the steering column to reach the solenoid underneath, then crossed the terminals with his screwdriver; the engine started up. From somewhere, unbidden, came a shadow of unease. He stiffened and turned around.

"Do you hot-wire cars for living or is it a hobby, Mr. Markus?" said a strikingly beautiful woman frowning good-naturedly. Offering an apologetic smile, she handed him a plain white business card with a black dot inked in the center.

"Dottie's calling card," Avram said in a soft voice, all the while studying the woman carefully. She was wearing black pants and a black jacket. *Maybe silk, maybe man-made.* As she leaned forward to hand him the card, Markus noticed a 9mm Beretta pistol hanging from a shoulder holster under the jacket.

"I'm an old man," he muttered. "What does the deputy director of the CIA want?"

"Ms. Schreck is no longer deputy director. Director Gervaise was killed last night in a break-in. Ms. Schreck is his replacement." The woman flashed her ID. "My name is Agent A'isha Khouri. My friends call me Alie. I've been dispatched to fetch you to headquarters *today.*" He saw a gleam of amusement light up her eyes. "I'm instructed to use my charms or my Beretta—whatever works. I have a rented car and a private airplane waiting to fly you to Washington for a twelve o'clock meeting."

Avram wasn't listening. He rubbed a hand over the back of his neck and exhaled wearily. He felt lightheaded and confused. *Paranoid Phillip Gervaise killed in a suspicious break-in.* He knew better.

A soft, humid breeze ruffled the tops of the palm trees along Seaway Drive. In the distance he could hear the rumble of a freight train. Somewhere close by, a church bell tolled the hour. Eight o'clock.

THE GULFSTREAM 550 JET cruised silently at 450 miles per hour above Cape Canaveral. Avram studied the cabin's sparkling off-white interior, tan leather recliner seats, plush beige carpeting, and teak trim. He nodded approvingly to Alie Khouri seated across the narrow aisle. "The CIA has upgraded its travel class."

"Your tax dollars at work," she said. Her slim fingers absently massaged a teardrop-shaped necklace that hung from her neck, brushing the swell of her breasts.

"Is that pendant Middle Eastern?"

"My father gave it to me. One side is engraved *Ayat-al-Kursi*, which are verses of protection, and the other side reads *Surah al-Ikhlas*—"

Avram cut in. " 'Oneness of God.' I speak Arabic."

She raised her eyebrows.

The copilot ambled down the aisle and handed Markus a phone. "Call for you, sir."

"Checking to see you are safely in our clutches, Avram, dear," Schreck said.

"Your beautiful Muslim bounty hunter tracked me down."

"Don't underestimate Alie," Schreck cautioned.

"The girl is not the issue. You don't understand, Dottie. I'm burned out."

"A crisis is unraveling. Few people have your experience and connections."

"No thanks. I was over retirement age when Gervaise assigned me the Hassan extraction; then he quashed Hassan's testimony because it embarrassed the Saudis. I'm out of the game. I can barely walk without—"

She cut him off. "Get over it, Avram. This is serious shit." Then she hung up.

Muneer Hassan, he mused.

12

THE MARCH WEATHER WAS COLD AND RAINY. Dr. Asif Sajjad left the Kahuta Research Laboratory precisely at seven o'clock, as was his habit. While running Pakistan's nuclear program, Sajjad had become a millionaire selling construction blueprints for centrifuges to enrich uranium and uranium hexafluoride, essential raw materials used in making nuclear weapons. His customers included Libya, Iran and North Korea. U.S. intelligence had learned Sajjad was not only selling atomic secrets, but that his aides were privately meeting with Osama bin Laden.

Sajjad pulled up his collar. He opened a large black umbrella to shield him from the windblown rain and picked his way along the crowded pavement towards his Mercedes Maybach 62S in the parking area. In the near-darkness the nuclear scientist bumped an old man hobbling with the use of a cane. Sajjad scowled at the Pashtun peasant, cursing him for his clumsiness.

A few minutes later, Dr. Asif Sajjad sat behind the wheel of his Mercedes scratching at what he thought was an insect bite on his leg. A wave of dizziness hit him as he tried to maneuver the car key into the ignition switch opening. Gurgling sounds escaped his lips. Sajjad struggled to find his cell phone. His face was bathed in sweat from the exertion. Choking and unable to breathe, the father of Pakistan's nuclear bomb clawed at his chest as the deadly scorpion venom coursed through his bloodstream.

"I COMMEND YOU ON THE SAJJAD PROJECT," Phillip Gervaise said from his desk safely seven thousand miles away at Langley.

Avram did not respond. He took no pleasure from the act of killing, only a sense of professional accomplishment.

"We have another assignment."

"Get somebody else. I'm past mandatory retirement age."

Gervaise ignored the protest. "Next to bin Laden, a Saudi named Muneer Hassan is at the top of our 'bad guys' list. Hassan was behind the attack on the *U.S.S. Cole* in October of 2000. We suspect he's also one of the masterminds of the 9-11 bombing. The guy is part of bin Laden's brain trust—second or third in command."

Avram sighed heavily. "What do you want from me?"

"An extraction. Muneer Hassan is a high-value target. I want you to handle a CT operation." Avram was familiar with the agency lingo for the practice known as extraordinary rendition. The letters stood for "collection and transfer," snatching suspected terrorists from a foreign country and holding them in American custody.

"Pakistan intelligence reports Hassan is holed up in the Faisalabad area. After this, for all I care, you can retire and start a fucking scorpion farm." Gervaise's voice hardened. "I don't want to know how you do it, but make it happen; we need the intel." The CIA director chuckled. "And capturing Hassan would be a coup for the agency."

FATIMA JINNAH PARK IN ISLAMABAD was crowded at noon. After Pakistan gained independence in 1947, its military leaders had decided to create a new capital city that would be easier to control than Karachi, the original capital. The result was Islamabad, a million-person city that Pakistanis called Isloo.

Hundreds of Islooites thronged the park, walking, jogging and enjoying the natural greenery. Avram sat on a bench, his cane resting by his side. He watched children flying kites and cavorting on colorful swings; their high-pitched laughter reminded him of another time, another place and another child—long buried.

A short olive-skinned man with a military bearing approached. *"Assalam Alaikum."*

"How are you? *Ap kaise hai,*" Avram replied in Urdu.

"When the lights are on, the fountain and the Baradari sculpture are breathtaking."

Avram looked at the man; his hair was nearly black and shot with gray at the temples. The eyes were a penetrating blue with deep fissures around them.

"Thank you for agreeing to see me, General Kayani."

"Your president offered two billion in additional military aid as an incentive for us to forcefully rid our country of terrorists. It would have been churlish to do otherwise. You have come a long way, surely not without good reason. How may I render assistance?"

"How far is Faisalabad?"

General Alam Kayani took a deep breath. "Ah. So this is to be the purpose of our meeting? The distance I can give you: one hundred and fifty miles south of Islamabad."

Avram lowered his voice. "My assignment is to capture and extract Muneer Hassan—alive. The CIA believes you know where he is in hiding. We Americans have an expression: 'You can catch more flies with honey than with vinegar.' "

The general steepled his fingers and pressed them tightly to his lips. "The honey is?"

"Five million dollars."

General Kayani nodded his head slowly. "And the vinegar?"

"Dr. Asif Sajjad's sudden death was a tragedy."

Kayani tilted his head slightly and smiled; he found the threat mildly amusing. "Unfortunately, Dr. Sajjid feathered his own nest. In Pakistan this is not uncommon. Even in America your politicians take bribes and *baksheesh*; you call them political contributions— and your high court approves the practice. As to Asif Sajjad, thanks to him, Pakistan now has the means to protect our nation against the threat of nuclear blackmail from neighboring India or China." He paused, his eyes narrowing. "Perhaps we should take a lesson from Israel and call Pakistan's nuclear deterrent our Delilah Option."

He stood. "Surely you can put aside your arrogance and walk with me a bit. The children's sounds mask eavesdropping from parabolic microphones—one never knows." Kayani laughed. "The famous CIA assassin, the Scorpion, visits in person to appeal to my greed—and to threaten my life?

"I do not lust after your CIA bribe money, nor am I fearful of your threats. I served as commander of the Black Storks commando division of the Pakistan Army for five years; I don't frighten easily. I am willing to help you because I want Muneer Hassan and his ilk out of my country. *Farshteyn?*"

Avram permitted himself a rare smile. "*Ich farshteyn*," he replied in Yiddish. "I understand."

...13

"HOW DID YOU FIND HASSAN?" Avram asked.

"The usual way," Kayani told him. "A friend of a friend of an enemy—and money." The general stood well back from the window of the Crescent textile mills. "Hassan made a call from Faisalabad to an al-Qaeda cell in Yemen. We tracked him through a monitored telephone intercept." Avram heard the general's hearty laugh. "We offered a financial *incentive* and within hours a *friend* reported a local cab driver told him Hassan was traveling in disguise as a burka-clad woman." He pointed. "The man is hiding in that two-story safe house on Sargodha Road."

"How many men do you have?"

"A dozen Black Storks; they will be sufficient."

Avram glanced at the luminous dial on his watch: 11 p.m. He knew they would have a tactical advantage waiting until just before midnight to conduct the raid, but this was tribal Pakistan; everybody was related. It was only a matter of time before the terrorist learned the Pakistani general was tracking him. Avram couldn't let Hassan slip away.

Kayani handled the briefing. Around him crouched ten hard-looking, olive-skinned soldiers and two officers, all dressed in dark combat uniforms. On their left shoulders each wore the Black Stork insignia: winged dragons and lightning bolts.

"I want to overwhelm the people in the house and create confusion," Kayani said. "Synchronize your watches. It is 23:10. We move out at 23:30. Colonel Mitha, your team will handle the main

56

assault, breaking through the front door and firing gas grenades. Captain Mehmood, have your men circle around the house; wait for the occupants to try and escape through the back entrance. Mr. Markus will accompany your group."

He passed around a photograph of a round-faced man with a full head of black hair, a beard, and large ears, wearing glasses. "The Americans want this man alive. As far as any others in the building, if they have weapons…" He shrugged. "Defend yourselves."

Avram noted that each of the Black Storks carried an HK-MP5 submachine gun, as well as a Heckler & Koch pistol for backup. Avram carried the CIA's standard issue handgun, the Browning 9 mm with a fifteen-round magazine.

At precisely 23:30, General Kayani stepped into the moonlight, raised his hand and motioned his men forward. The Black Storks pulled on gas masks, grabbed their weapons and moved out silently. The two biggest men carried a knocker, a thick steel pipe with handles attached. A few minutes later Avram heard the sound of shattering wood and yelling as Colonel Mitha's men burst through the front door.

Captain Mehmood's team raced across the flat open field. Dark figures appeared in the upper windows of the house as Avram approached the rear of the building. He heard the stuttering recoil of automatic fire. Captain Mehmood stumbled, his arms opened wide, and he fell forward. Mehmood's men returned fire blindly in the darkness, long ear-splitting bursts on full automatic that shattered windows.

Avram raised his Browning and firing a four-shot burst at the shooter, trying to push the man away from the window. He paused for a moment, mind racing, breath ragged. Suddenly gunfire was coming from the back. A shadowy figure rose to one knee, firing at the Black Stork team. Avram fired another burst. The gunfire blew the man off his feet.

Inside the house, a man shouted, *"Allahu akbar! Allahu akbar!"* Another long burst from an automatic weapon ripped through the night.

Avram scrambled to his feet and rushed to the back door. He listened for more gunfire, but only heard loud voices. The Black Storks were yelling at one another in Punjabi as they cleared rooms on the second floor. In the brief calm that followed, the lights inside flickered on. The smoke was thinning; the action had eased. The back door was locked. Avram lashed out his foot and it crashed open. He ripped off his mask and slipped through the doorway, catching a glimpse through the haze of a bearded man with an Uzi leveled at him.

"Drop the gun, Hassan!" Avram yelled, knowing his Browning was no match for the terrorist's Uzi. Muneer Hassan fired two quick bursts. The first thudded into the wall above him. Avram half dove, half fell, grunting in pain as the second round pounded into his right thigh, snapping the femur. He saw his blood puddling on the floor. Hassan stood over him, unsmiling, his finger poised on the trigger.

A voice interrupted. "It is over," Kayani said. "Lower your weapon and live."

Hassan turned, prepared to fire. Before he could pull the trigger, he was shot in the thigh, the testicle and the stomach with rounds from an AK-47 Russian assault rifle.

"Don't kill him!" Avram whispered, and then he blacked out.

AT THE AL-RAAZI HOSPITAL on Satyana Road, doctors kept a close watch over two special patients. Black Stork troopers patrolled the corridors in twenty-four-hour shifts, preventing press access and guarding both the prisoner and the wounded CIA operative.

General Kayani grunted unhappily as he sat by Avram's bedside reviewing the raid. "Six terrorist suspects were in the house.

Five are dead. We took four casualties: two dead, and Captain Mehmood was seriously wounded. His army days are past."

Avram sat up in bed. "Is Hassan fit enough to travel?"

Alam Kayani stood up to leave. He shrugged. "That is for the
doctors to decide. I do not wish to hear of your CIA secret prisons."
He shook hands with Avram. "A broken femur is a career-ender,
even for the famous Scorpion. You have two screws in your knee
and one in your hip. Go home, my friend."

Avram nodded. "By the way, Alam, thanks for saving my life."

"DID YOU SEARCH HASSAN?" Avram asked Blakeslee
Lane, the six-foot tall, dark-eyed, clean-shaven, black assistant CIA
station chief in Islamabad.

"Two bank cards. Hassan had access to Saudi and Kawaiti bank
accounts. Doesn't that strike you as a tad strange for an al-Qaeda
operative? They normally use the *hawala* worldwide money-trans-
mission system: money transferred by phone or fax between dealers
in different countries with a code number. It's fast and undetectable."

"You have your sat phone?" Avram asked.

Lane nodded.

"Tell Gervaise to fly somebody over from Johns Hopkins today. I want Hassan patched up and out of Pakistan in forty-eight
hours before his lawyers show up on CNN. We'll move him to
Camp Chapman in Afghanistan. There's an airfield at our Salerno
base, a few minutes away from Chapman."

...14

MUNEER HASSAN HOWLED IN ARABIC and blinked furiously. Tears streamed down his cheeks from the pain of traveling in a van on rough terrain. His wounds were healing, but it was too soon to remove all of the stitches. They had given him pills to ease the discomfort and then put a black hood on him. A plane had carried him somewhere.

"How do you want to handle the interrogation?" Blakeslee Lane asked. "The lawyers in Washington approve everything: sleep deprivation, waterboarding, temperature extremes, loud music, cramped confinement. The Geneva Convention don't mean shit to politicians who haven't got kids in the service in harm's way."

Avram rubbed his aching thigh and shook his head. "There's a better way. After 9-11 the CIA got approval for use of sodium pentothal on prisoners." He winked. "When public safety is at risk. With Hassan's injuries, he's in a weakened condition. Pentothal may make him more compliant. When one's higher cortical functions are suppressed, lying is more difficult than telling the truth. Pentothal makes subjects chatty and cooperative with interrogators." He paused. "The problem is that the reliability of statements made under thiopental can be questionable. Blakeslee, I want you to videotape Hassan's interrogation—every word."

Avram downed two hydrocodone tablets to moderate the constant pain. "Find an Arab-speaking nurse or medic to give Hassan his first dose. If he asks where he is, have them say he has been transferred to a Saudi prison—nothing more. Then give Hassan something that will make him sleep for ten hours."

THE RIYADH CONSPIRACY

THE FOLLOWING MORNING, MUNEER HASSAN was led into a ten-by-twelve cinderblock room with windowless walls and a single naked bulb overhead. Blakeslee Lane videotaped through the one-way glass from the adjoining room. Hassan appeared slightly glassy-eyed. He didn't complain as Avram pushed him into a chair and snapped shackles around his legs. Only then did Avram uncuff him and tug off his hood. Muneer Hassan blinked, then opened and closed his hands.

"Muneer Hassan," Avram said, continuing in Arabic. "We captured you in Faisalabad, put you on a plane, and now you're in what we call a secret undisclosed location in Saudi Arabia. We Saudis are experienced in dealing with your kind of al-Qaeda scum."

Hassam's eyes widened. He took a deep breath and sighed in relief rather than fear. "*Al-Hamdulillah, al-Hamdulillah.* Praise Allah," he said, his wide lips spreading into a rubbery grin. "Please to call these important personages." From memory, Hassan volunteered four telephone numbers. "Prince Khalid bin Abdul Al-Aziz is King Abdullah's nephew. He will vouch for me and give you instructions."

For a moment Avram was speechless. He paused. The room was silent; the only sound was the faint buzzing of the light bulb. Somewhere outside a dog barked. "Don't lie, Hassan. If you lie—"

"It's true. Please. You will see. I have important connections in Saudi Arabia. Prince Khalid met with al-Qaeda in 1991 and agreed to provide substantial secret funds in exchange for bin Laden's pledge to refrain from promoting *jihad* in the kingdom."

Hassan seemed serious. Avram wondered where this was leading. "You are impressing me, Muneer. And in Pakistan, do you also have important connections?"

The terrorist grinned. "A high-ranking military officer, Air Chief Marshal Mushaf Suleman, a man with close ties to Muslims inside Pakistan's Inter-Services Intelligence—the ISI." Hassan seemed to be tiring.

"Go on, Muneer," Avram prodded. "How do you know this?"

Hassan said proudly, "Bin Laden personally told me he struck a deal with the air chief marshal to get protection, arms and supplies for al-Qaeda. Bin Laden told me the arrangements were blessed by the Saudis."

"Who knew about 9-11?"

"Nine-eleven changed nothing between the Saudis, Pakistanis and al-Qaeda. Prince Aziz knew about the forthcoming attacks on American targets on September eleventh; he remained silent for fear of revealing the secret Saudi arrangements."

"Besides Prince Aziz, whose telephone numbers did you give us?"

"Prince Turki al Saud and Prince Fahd bin Turki, other relatives of the king."

Avram banged his fist on the table. "I think you are lying to save your skin. You are a ghost: a detainee whose existence the United States will not confirm to outsiders, like lawyers or families or human rights monitors."

Hassam had difficulty staying awake. In almost a whisper he said, "I attended a meeting in Kandahar with Prince Turki and Taliban officials. Turki promised more aid would flow to the Taliban and the Saudis would never ask for bin Laden's extradition, so long as al-Qaeda kept its promise to direct fundamentalism away from the kingdom."

"How were the funds sent from Saudi Arabia to al-Qaeda? Answer me!"

"Through the three royal prince intermediaries that I named. I gave you their private telephone numbers—call them."

Avram turned to the one-way mirror and motioned with his fingers, cutting across his throat for Lane to stop videotaping.

"JESUS CHRIST!" SPUTTERED PHILLIP GERVAISE. "We checked out the phone numbers—they are all legitimate. If Hassan's story leaks out, it will set off a major international flap and strain relations with our major oil supplier. Put the videotape in today's embassy pouch; address it to my attention marked 'Confidential—Urgent.' There will be no copies made, or it will be your ass, Markus. That's an order."

...15

Washington, D.C.
December 12, 2007

CIA Destroyed Tape Showing Interrogations

Washington Post—The Central Intelligence Agency in 2005 destroyed at least one videotape documenting the interrogation of an al-Qaeda operative in the agency's custody, a step it took in the midst of Congressional and legal scrutiny about its secret detention program, according to current and former government officials.

The videotape showed agency operatives in 2002 interrogating terrorism suspect Muneer Hassan. In a statement to employees on Thursday, Phillip Gervaise, the CIA director, said that the decision to destroy the tapes was made "within the CIA" and that they were destroyed to protect the safety of undercover officers and because they no longer had intelligence value.

The destruction of the tapes raises questions about whether agency officials withheld information from Congress, the courts and the Sept. 11 commission.

PART II

THE SCORPION

We're not in the Boy Scouts. If we'd wanted to be in the Boy Scouts, we could have joined the Boy Scouts.

Richard Helms
Former CIA Director

...16

WITH BLUE LIGHTS PULSATING, the state policeman conveyed Avram Markus and A'isha Khouri from the private airport to a location near Tyson's Corner in McLean, Virginia. To Avram, the complex looked like a modern suburban office park.

"This is Liberty Crossing," Alie said. "The building on the left houses the National Counter-Terrorism Center. The other high-rise is the office of the director of national intelligence."

Markus ignored her comment. "I'm starved."

The trooper smiled. "We passed a McDonald's on the corner."

Alie grimaced. "We will be late."

"What will they do, fire me?"

"FILL ME IN ON THIS GUY," Campbell said, glancing at his watch. "It's 12:30—he's late."

"Born in Israel," Dorothy Schreck commented, "on a kibbutz near Qiryat Shemona in the middle of the Jezreel Valley in the Lower Galilee—"

"Near Megiddo?" Campbell interrupted.

She nodded. "Now you know why Markus can't turn us down. He served in an elite branch of the Israeli army, the Sayeret Matkal, before joining Mossad. It was rumored Avram was one of the leaders in the Wrath of God Operation—hunting down and assassinating members of the Palestinian Liberation Organization's Black September Organization in revenge for the massacre of Jewish athletes at the Munich Olympics."

Campbell's eyebrows rose; he listened attentively.

"Avram emigrated from Israel in 1985 amid rumors. Some said he resigned in protest over Prime Minister Shamir's overtures to Russia. Others said it was something else. Bill Casey was our CIA director at time. He took a liking to Markus and brought him into the Agency. After that, everything should be in his Agency dossier."

Campbell picked up the blue folder, opened it and scowled. "It's empty. Someone's purged it. What the hell's going on?"

The light on Campbell's phone flashed amber. "They are in the lobby," his secretary announced.

One wall of the National Intelligence Center lobby was lined with photographs of terrorist attacks perpetuated against the United States. Avram studied a plaque beside the pictures; it read "Never Again." The words were also Israel's unofficial motto, growing out of the conviction that the Holocaust justified any measures to ensure its survival so Jews would *never again* be led as lambs to the slaughter. As he read the familiar words, his stomach tightened and he had an uncomfortable premonition—fear.

"THANK YOU FOR ALMOST BEING ON TIME," Campbell said sarcastically as he grasped Avram's outstretched hand in a vise-like grip. He was surprised to feel it returned in kind. Campbell scrutinized the veteran operative and was unimpressed. Avram Markus usually managed to look slightly lost and distracted. Those who didn't know him tended to underestimate him, a quality that served him well in the field.

Avram looked around Campbell's office. The early afternoon sun filtered through the tinted, bulletproof glass windows. The furniture was generically bureaucratic: a mahogany desk and three tan leather chairs.

He put his arm around Schreck's shoulder and hugged her. A tear crept into the corner of her eye. "Long time," she said. He studied his old friend. She had developed a network of tiny wrinkles and lines around the eyes.

"And thank you, Agent Khouri," Campbell added with a chuckle, "for digging up this old Scorpion. You are excused."

"She stays," Markus said.

"No way," Campbell stammered. "This agent is not cleared for—"

"If she goes, I go." He stood up to leave.

Campbell's countenance darkened. He glared at Dorothy Schreck, who shrugged her shoulders. "I'll vouch for Agent Khouri."

Avram observed dark shadows under Campbell's eyes, a film of sweat on his forehead. The DNI took a deep breath. He glared at Markus. "Why are you spreading unsubstantiated rumors about Phillip Gervaise?"

Avram Markus reached into his backpack and pulled out two black objects. He tossed them on Campbell's desk. "This is a copy of the videotape Gervaise destroyed rather than turn it over to the 9-11 commission."

The room was silent.

He picked up the other object and pressed a switch. A red light flickered. Campbell stared at the device. "What in the hell is that thing?"

"To make sure you're not recording me."

"A jamming device."

"When you work in this wilderness of mirrors as long as I did, you learn to protect yourself. Until Gervaise was killed, this video-tape was my life insurance policy." He paused. "Any coffee?"

Campbell pressed the intercom and gave instructions.

Markus was tired; his back ached. "A top aide of bin Laden named Muneer Hassan was captured in Pakistan. I used a thiopental sodium drip to get him to talk and videotaped the interrogation. The prisoner reeled off the home and mobile phone numbers of the Saudi king's nephew, Prince Khalid bin Aziz, who was a pal of the American president at the time. Under the truth serum, Hassan told me Khalid was responsible for channeling funds to bin Laden and that the prince knew about 9-11 before it happened—but kept quiet."

"Why didn't you speak up, man?" Campbell demanded.

"Avram would have ended up in Leavenworth," Schreck explained, "for breaking his confidentiality agreement."

Joseph Campbell grimaced. "Director Schreck thinks you can help us. I heard you were a military hero years ago. Of your record, I'm respectful. But that was then, and this is now. To me you look like a worn-out old man."

"I agree completely." Avram smiled thinly. "So why am I here?"

Campbell's secretary brought in coffee. No one spoke until she left.

The director of national intelligence wiped his sweaty forehead. "Truth be told, we need any help we can get." He took a deep breath. "We have information that an attack is planned by Iran against Israel—involving nuclear weapons."

Markus felt hollowness in the pit of his stomach, his body tensing involuntarily. He willed himself to remain calm and silent.

"It is our intelligence assessment, supported by British MI-6, that with Chinese and North Korean help, Iran now has short-range missile delivery capabilities. What we don't know is if they have the nuclear warheads to mount on them."

Avram felt a vague panic. He slowly sipped his coffee.

Schreck said, "If they are not already producing fissionable material, Iran may be purchasing warheads from arms merchants or from the arsenal of some nuclear country, such as Russia."

"Do you know the timeframe?"

Schreck looked at Agent Khouri. Alie said, "On the Islamic calendar, 1432 is *Eid al-Adha,* an important religious holiday for all Muslims commemorating Ibrahim's willingness to sacrifice his son as an act of obedience to Allah."

Avram looked into the cup of coffee. "And when is *Eid al-Adha?*"

"That's the problem," Schreck said. "November fifth—four days from now."

With narrowed eyes Avram stared at his friend. "What else haven't you told me?"

"One of the three target areas is Magiddo."

Avram Markus was burned out, and he knew it. For a long while he was silent. Finally he smiled the tolerant smile of a man who knew he had no choice. "You took me through all the proper stages, didn't you, Dottie? Right up to the target being within range of my kibbutz, Neot Mordechai. All the right buttons pushed?"

"Was there any other way to do it?"

"I suppose you wouldn't be sitting in that chair if there were." He exhaled slowly.

Campbell said, "President Kennan demands verifiable proof of the alleged attack. Dorothy tells me you have a relationship with Pyotr Zhukov, who now lives in New York. The old general maintains high-level contacts within the Russian military. He would know if bombs are being outsourced."

Schreck added, "Avram, we need you back in the field—in Israel. Prime Minister Chpindel is your old friend and comrade. It is in our national interest to know Israel's intentions; there can be no unpleasant surprises. We have enough on our plate as it is."

Anger was counterproductive. Avram entered a state of operational calm, thinking, *Momentum is important.* He suspected the intelligence establishment was still hamstrung with ass-covering and political meddling. He had spent too many years observing CIA leaks and indiscretions to trust anybody. "I will operate in my own way and make my own decisions. I have no profile, no publicity, nothing. I want no crowding, no bird-dogging, no paper trails of any kind."

Campbell exclaimed, "That's not acceptable. We are a team—"

Avram shot him a stone-cold glare. "Take it or leave it."

"We accept," Schreck said, ignoring her red-faced superior.

IN THE ASH LIGHT OF LATE AFTERNOON, Markus called a cab and was driven to downtown Washington. At Seventh Street, he paid the driver and walked, keeping his eyes on passersby. It was a tradecraft habit he needed to resharpen. He purchased two cell phones and a lined raincoat, then walked to the Red Roof Inn on H Street.

Registering under the name F. Pierce, he ordered coffee and a grilled cheese sandwich to be sent to the room, paying in cash. He took an ice-cold shower, dug out his address book, squinting to read his own handwriting, and punched in a private number.

In Brighton Beach the phone was answered. *"Da."*

In Russian, Markus said, "I need to talk to Zhukov. Is the old Cossack still alive?"

Markus heard mutterings. "Who wants to know?" a low, gravelly voice demanded.

"The Scorpion."

A long pause. "Russian baths; Tenth Street; noon." Click.

...17

MARKUS USED THE BACK STAIRWAY, slipped out of the hotel, cabbed to Union Station, and purchased a ticket for the 7 a.m. train to New York City. As was his custom, he settled into a seat in the last row. A few minutes later a soft, familiar voice said, "Is this seat taken? Schreck wants me to make sure you take your pills on time."

Avram looked at Alie Khouri, then squeezed the bridge of his nose and closed his eyes for a second. He knew he had lost the *edge*, the instinct agents need to take watchful care of themselves and survive. He took a deep breath, stood up, walked the length of the train compartment, and returned, fixing Alie with an ice-cold stare. "Is the man in the gray suit reading the *Wall Street Journal* one of yours?"

She looked startled. "No, of course not."

Markus limped stiffly back up the aisle, taking a seat next to the man. "Hello, my name is Avram," he said with a warm smile, leaning over to shake hands. When the surprised agent extended his arm, Markus's right hand shot out, grabbing the man's right index finger and forcing it back to the breaking point. A protest was hardly out of the agent's mouth when four rigid fingers jabbing into his solar plexus cut it off. He grunted in pain.

"Quiet," Avram hissed. "Answer my questions or your finger will be broken in three places. Understand?"

The man flushed, wide-eyed in pain, beads of sweat forming on his brow.

"Who sent you, Schreck or Campbell?" Avram increased the pressure.

"Campbell," he gasped.

Markus removed the agent's Glock 22 from the armpit holster under his left shoulder. "Leave the train at Wilmington. Tell your boss if he violates our understanding again, I'm history. Then Campbell can explain to the president how he fucked up the mission. *Capice?*"

The man rubbed his aching finger, nodding sullenly. His dark eyes flashed hatred.

"WE'LL GET OFF AT TRENTON," Avram said. "Campbell may have people at Penn Station." He shifted uncomfortably in the seat. His thigh was acting up. It had been a long time since Avram had put himself through this kind of activity. He wasn't sure he had it in him anymore.

He looked at the beautiful young woman sitting next to him and slowly felt the tension subside. Putting his palms together in front of his lips, he asked quietly, "Since you are to be my nanny, may I make you a proposition?"

She raised her eyebrows.

"I've always been a loner, operating independently; no paperwork, no partners, no risk-adverse bureaucrats looking over my shoulders. Dorothy overrates me. I'm too old; this Iranian threat is too important for me to try and go it alone." Avram allowed himself a tight smile. "I suggest that, instead of nursemaiding me and reporting to Schreck, you work *with* me. No contact with anyone without my approval."

She pursed her lips. "Why did you stand up for me in Campbell's office?"

He held up three fingers. "Schreck wouldn't send a minder for me that she doesn't trust one hundred percent. Second, you're a Muslim." He smiled thinly. "Muslims and Jews aren't welcome by the CIA hierarchy. They're never certain where our true loyalties lie. Therefore, you must be highly qualified."

"And the third reason?"

Avram hesitated. "You remind me of someone." She saw moisture creep into his eye. He brushed it away, sighed and said in a low voice, "Someone I lost a long time ago." He stared out of the window at the Maryland countryside hurtling by. The silence between them was punctuated by the metallic rumbling of the train on the tracks.

Alie touched Markus' forearm gently. "It wouldn't look good on my record if the legendary Scorpion failed a mission on my watch." She flashed a wide smile. "I don't want to go back to the ladies' shoe department in Nordstrom's." She offered her hand. "Count me in."

"Give me your driver's license," Avram said. He checked her photograph on the card. "Get two rooms at the Marriott Hotel in the Flower District near East 26th. Call El Al from the hotel room; use your personal credit card. Order two economy class tickets from Newark to Tel Aviv on tomorrow's afternoon flight. Can your credit limit handle a three-thousand-dollar charge?"

Greeted by silence, he handed her one of the Radio Shack cell phones. "Use this only to contact me—no one else." He paused. "Am I going too fast for you?"

She glowered and said nothing.

"I'll be at the Russian baths at noon."

FOR HALF AN HOUR AVRAM WANDERED from Penn Station along the busy shops on 32nd Street. He entered Macy's front entrance, browsed through the men's department checking mirrors for familiar reflections, then exited through the back entrance on West 34th Street, walking toward 6th Avenue. It appeared no one was following him, though from experience he knew expert watchers were almost impossible to detect.

He entered a small, musty bookstore, Judaica Treasures. "Pleasure to see you again, sir," the proprietor said. "Been a long time."

"A rush, rush job, Irving: two passports, two driver's licenses. Mine needs renewing, and my granddaughter requires a new one. Her name is Victoria."

Irving winked. "Pretty lady. Nice name."

For the first time in two days Avram permitted himself a smile. "How do you stay in business competing with Amazon's Kindle, e-books and the big book chains?"

Irving giggled. "I'm like Wal-Mart. I help people live better—and longer."

...18

THE RUSSIAN AND TURKISH BATHS BUILDING appeared uninviting from the outside. The worn-looking entrance area smelled gamey and musky. Approaching the front desk, Avram and Alie were greeted by a surly, barrel-chested man with a close-cropped gray beard and olive complexion. "You together?" he grumbled.

Avram nodded.

"Thirty each for admission, plus thirty-five for the *platza*."

"What's the *platza*?" Alie asked.

"You'll love it, lady," the bearded man said, ogling her breasts. "*Platza* is Jewish acupuncture. Our trained masseuse scrubs you with oak leaves soaked in natural oils, which opens your pores and removes toxins—"

Avram shook his head. "They beat you with a broom. Not a good idea."

The young woman bristled at his patronizing attitude. She reached in her pocketbook, ignored Avram, and handed over sixty-five dollars. "A good massage is just what I need."

The attendant grinned and placed two lock boxes on the counter, advising them to put their valuables in assigned lockers. From under the counter he withdrew shorts, robes, towels and flip-flops, then pointed the way to the dressing rooms.

Markus put on sandals and a robe that was three sizes too big. He shuffled back to the front counter. "Pyotr Zhukov?" he said.

The man's eyes widened. "He's in the Russian sauna."

WEARING SHORTS AND A TOWEL around his neck, Markus entered the rock-walled, two-hundred-degree Russian sauna. He felt the intense heat sear his nostrils and penetrate his lungs. A group of silent people huddled on a cement bench, dumping plastic buckets of ice-cold water over each other's heads to cool off. Women in string bikinis, towels and mud masks sat next to Hasids with *peyos* tucked behind their ears.

In the far corner two hulking figures sat apart from the others. Avram heard a short, barking chuckle. "*Tovarishch*," the Russian said.

"*Priyatno vas videt*," Markus replied. "Good to see you."

Pyotr Sergeyevich Zhukov was a bullet-shaped man of eighty with a wide, rolling body and bald, liver-spotted head. His bristly gray hair was cut short. By his side sat a linebacker-size bodyguard with thick gray sideburns and a grim, downturned mouth. Zhukov cocked a stubby finger at Markus, beckoning him to take a seat next to him.

"How can you stand this heat?" Avram gasped.

"There's no heat in here today," the Russian laughed. "I should put on a coat."

"With the fur covering your chest and back, I thought you were wearing one."

Zhukov chuckled. "*Vy delaete horoshuyu shutku.* You make a joke."

ALIE KHOURI ENTERED THE SAUNA draped only in her towel. A robust-looking 60-year-old Russian masseuse accompanied her. Zhukov elbowed Markus. "Watch. Boris put on good show."

The masseuse instructed Alie to lay face down on a plywood bench covered with a towel. Starting the *platza*, he gave Alie a whack across her upper back, driving her nose into a mouthful of sopping terry cloth. A cool wet towel was pressed over her head, forcing her to inhale mildew and astringent soap mixed with the scent of autumn leaves. Then Boris whipped away her towel and began to pummel Alie's bare body with a broom made of oak-leaf branches tied with string and soaked in olive oil soap.

She tried to get up, protesting, "It's too hot."

The masseuse smirked. "Someone call 911; the lady's too hot. I fix," he said, emptying a bucket of frigid water over her. He followed up by rubbing her skin with a grainy soap, twisting Alie into awkward positions for no reason other than to display her naked body to the appreciative audience. When it was over, Boris slapped Alie on her rump, lifted her from the table, and dragged her toward the frigid swimming pool. Even with her blotchy-red skin and drowned-rat hairdo, Avram could see that Alie Khouri was a truly exquisite woman.

As Boris prepared to dump Alie in the icy water, she grabbed the man's right arm and yanked it towards her right shoulder while pressing her left foot into his right hip. She held the surprised masseuse's wrist in a tight grip as she swiveled her naked pelvis against his elbow and applied pressure until it dislocated with a sharp popping sound. Then she turned Boris around and, with a kick to the small of his back, launched the screaming Russian into the pool.

Everyone whistled and applauded wildly. A'isha Khouri draped her towel rakishly over her shoulder, lifted her chin up, pulled her pelvis in, winked at Avram, and strutted out of the sauna.

Zhukov said, "Now that is what I call a great ass. You getting any, or are you married to your fist?" Avram's face darkened.

"No matter," Zhukov snickered. "We meet on roof. Private place to drink, eat *blinis* and talk. Just robe, no tapes, no wires, *ne ponimaet?*"

"*Ya vas panimayu.* I have no interest in spy toys. I come on serious business."

THE RUSSIAN WAS WAITING at the roof restaurant, sitting at a table in his white terry cloth robe. In the background hovered his heavy-shouldered, bald bodyguard. Zhukov drained the vodka glass with a flip of his wrist, stood up with a grunting noise, and clasped Markus in a bear hug. "All these years; suddenly you show up at my doorstep."

Avram smelled the alcohol on the former KGB general's breath—vodka. He knew that when a person's blood alcohol rose to a certain level, it emitted an odor into the lungs.

Pyotr Sergeyevich Zhukov ruled the *Organizatsiya* in Brighton Beach. After immigrating to America, he had reorganized the Russian Mafia into a multi-million-dollar enterprise with a hierarchy similar to the Italian Mafia's, with whom he did business.

Zhukov snatched a cigar from a box on the table. He bit off the end and lit it. After several heavy puffs, he looked at Markus with a faint smile. "You had many admirers at Moscow Center. Tell me, are you still in the great game?"

"There's word of a crisis brewing in the Middle East."

The Russian grunted in agreement. "There is always a crisis brewing in that desert graveyard of oil." The topic had been broached. Now both men would proceed carefully.

Zhukov flicked a cigar ash on the concrete floor. "In '84 you read the tea leaves well. Shamir was a fool to trust Russia."

"And you read them as well. Now you are the tsar of Brighton Beach. Had you remained in Russia, they would have disposed of you like they did General Lebed."

"Alexander Lebed was stupid to grant an interview with *60 Minutes*."

Markus pressed, "Before Lebed died in that mysterious helicopter crash in 2002, he claimed that after the dissolution of the Soviet Union, hundreds of nuclear weapons were floating around, no longer under the control of the armed forces of Russia."

Zhukov shrugged. "It was a confusing period."

"Pyotr, you were in command of the 13th GUMO. Your unit had responsibility for controlling nuclear weapons in Chelyabinsk Province and protecting the Mayak Chemical Combine Nuclear Facility." Avram narrowed his eyes. "Could Russian nuclear bombs have gotten into Iranian hands? It is important that I know."

The Russian said dismissively, "Don't talk nonsense; we are too old. A nuclear explosion in the Middle East is bad for my business, but good business for your military-industrial complex: new bombers, new aircraft carriers, new tanks, new jobs, and more satellites that fire missiles. Enough foreplay. *Gavorit mne.* Tell me your story."

"The CIA believes Iran is preparing to attack Israel using nuclear bombs."

The Russian whistled. "This is more WMD bullshit."

When Avram didn't respond, the Russian sighed. "When I was commander of 13th GUMO, I lived in the godforsaken city of Ozerrzk surrounded by nothing but checkpoints, barbed wire, and ice. The place was called Chelyabinsk-65. Bombs were stored in warehouses protected by cheap padlocks and guards who, more often than not, didn't show up. It would have been simple for greedy officers wanting to make money to connect with arms dealers, Arabs, anybody."

Avram studied the Russian's eyes.

"When nuclear weapons were moved out of my warehouses, I had rules: work was to be performed by two men, plus a third who was supposed to be watching on camera. But sometimes they got drunk or sloppy, and they could pick their own partners, so you know the story."

He downed another drink in one gulp, his head tilted a little. Like many Russians, Zhukov saw life as a series of meaningless events to be laughed at. "These are only rumors, mind you, but word has it…" He winked. "A few bombs disappeared from the Chelyabinsk-65 inventory." He motioned to the waiter for another round of vodka.

"Were the bombs destined for Iran?"

Zhukov pointed a stubby finger. "Have your Jew agents check shipments from Kaliningrad destined for Algeria or some other phony destination."

"What shipping line?"

"Who knows? I'm not a dock master."

"Listen carefully to me, Pyotr. If the Jewish State is attacked by Iranian missiles carrying Russian warheads, I guarantee you the Israelis will counter-strike, not only against Tehran, but as they threatened to in 1973, missiles will land in Red Square."

The Russian's bushy eyebrows lifted. "Moscow?"

"You know the horrific damage an Israeli Jericho-3 missile with a 10-kiloton warhead can do. Why would the Kremlin permit nuclear bombs to be shipped to Iran?"

Zhukov sucked in his breath. "Why? To resurrect the glory of the Soviet Union and make money." He paused. "Iran is pivotal in Russian thinking. It's the gateway to the Middle East. What's more, a close relationship with Iran lessens the likelihood that their mullahs will support the fucking rebels in Chechnya." He laughed a coarse laugh, toppling over his glass. "Like all of Europe, Mother Russia is in danger of Islamization."

Zhukov's shoulders sagged. "Officials turn their heads and are paid off by arms merchants or Islamists from Iran or anywhere." He sneered. "So Russian politicians are paid off. Is it any different in America?"

"Pyotr, from one old broken down warrior to another," Avram said with a failed attempt at a smile, "can you help me?"

"Tell your overrated ex-employer, the Mossad, to trace the goddamn shipment." The Russian wobbled to his feet, adding, "This conversation never happened."

MARKUS POSITIONED HIMSELF IN A DESERTED storefront on Avenue A. On his cell phone, he punched in a random series of numbers from memory, all the while scanning the street around him. In the old days he would have had a sweeper or two trailing after him to make sure he was clean and tidy up after him if he wasn't. *That was then and this is now*, he mused as the phone rang.

"Jewish Heritage Travel, *Shalom*."

"My field number is twenty-seven-ten. Check your files—it's been a while."

The woman's manner changed to brisk and efficient. "One moment, please."

A terse voice answered, "Hammerman."

"My name is Avram Markus, code name Scorpion."

"The man scoffed. "Excuse my bluntness, sir, but anyone can telephone and—"

"I haven't time to play spy games with you, son. Israel's security is at stake. I need to contact the Office with an urgent encrypted message, and I need to do it *now*. Send it and keep your mouth shut, or you will spend the rest of your Mossad career guarding a kibbutz garbage dump. *Ata meiveen otee?*"

"Yes, sir. *Heivantee hakol.* I understand."

"Send this message: 'To Director Mossad. Tell Chpindel nuclear bombs may be enroute by ship from Kaliningrad, Russia to Iran. I am returning on first flight.' Sign the message, 'Avram Markus, Scorpion.' "

"Holy shit!" Hammerman gulped.

...19

THE PRESIDENT DRUMMED HIS FINGERS on the conference table. All six members of his security staff were present: Campbell, director of national intelligence; Politto, secretary of state; Fishman, secretary of defense; Chairman of the Joint Chiefs Admiral Baysinger; Vice President Landry; and Dorothy Schreck representing the CIA.

"Bring us up to speed, Joseph."

Campbell's face reddened. "I regret to report that at 2 a.m. this morning, London time, Mr. Zakariya, the Iranian who warned us of the Iranian nuclear attack, was murdered in his hotel room." The veins bulged out in Campbell's neck as he added, "The assassin scrawled a message in blood on the wall that said, 'Death to American spies.'"

Dorothy Schreck noticed the president's jaw tighten. She guessed the wear and tear of the last few days was taking its toll. Dogged circles ringed Kennan's eyes; his hands appeared to tremble.

"If the Iranian spoke the truth, we only have three days left. Three days," Kennan repeated, gritting his teeth. "This nightmare scenario puts us between a rock and a hard place. If we announce that we believe an attack is imminent, all hell will break loose, including, I'm afraid, Israel's Samson Option. If we remain silent, possibly thousands of Israelis will die, plus an untold number of Americans traveling in the area."

Sanfred Fishman spoke. "Sir. I think we should adopt a posture of neutrality and distance ourselves as Israel's ally. Any preemptive military action by Israel will dramatically increase the price of crude oil—send it through the roof and put the world into recession.

Planes would be grounded; electricity and fertilizer would double or triple in price. Middle-class Americans and Europeans would be squeezed and—"

Kennan breathed a long sigh that came out sounding both worried and annoyed. "OK, Sandy, that's enough. We get the picture."

"One other point," Fishman added. "I know it sounds harsh, but if a nuclear showdown is inevitable in the Middle East, whether Israel starts it as a retaliatory strike, or Iran acts insane, my advice is to stand clear of it. When the smoke settles, it will be China, Russia and the United States moving in to grab the oil."

Joseph Campbell had trouble keeping his temper in check. "I would try my damnedest to avoid the catastrophe, rather than planning to profit for its aftermath."

Dorothy Schreck said, "If Israel were to strike first, America will face the threat of retaliation in the form of increased terrorism. It would be prudent to have our embassies worldwide placed on a high state of alert."

"Already done," said Cassia Politto. "We issued a secret communication this morning, giving no specifics." She paused, nervously fingering her glasses.

Kennan turned to his secretary of state. "Cassia, you want to add something?"

"Mr. President, my background is as an academic. For that reason, I understand the Iranian mullahs might be a gang of ranting demagogues, but Persia is one of the world's oldest civilizations; the Iranians are not stupid. They are well aware of Israel's massive retaliatory capability."

"And your point is?" Kennan snapped.

"My point, sir, is that we may be rushing to judgment about Iran."

Kennan brushed her comment aside impatiently. "We're rushing to Judgment Day, that's where the hell we are rushing to, and we only have a handful of days left. Of course we must do everything in our power to prevent this attack from happening. At the same time, it is my sworn duty to protect American lives. Zakariya paid with his life for trying to warn us. If we believe the man's information was correct, we must restrict travel and inform the public."

Finally, Kennan turned to Landry. "What do you think, C.J.?"

"While I don't subscribe to Sandy's doomsday scenario, I think he makes a point. When Iran's President Hanoush called for Israel to be wiped off the map and pursued a hard line on their nuclear program, I thought the man wanted to get reelected and was appealing to popular prejudices. However, my friend Reverend Isaiah Bowman has convinced me Hanoush is a true religious zealot who believes he has been chosen by Allah to hasten the coming of the Islamic messiah by launching a final holy war against the Jews. This makes him the type of lunatic who could push the button. I think we need to be prepared." Turning to Admiral Baysinger, he asked, "Jeb, what assets do we have for the removal of American citizens by sea?"

"Our Fifth Fleet was based in Bahrain; now it is temporarily in Qatar. The Sixth Fleet is headquartered in Naples, Italy, with 40 ships, 175 aircraft and 21,000 people—"

Kennan broke in. "How long will it take to evacuate our people and get your ships a safe distance away?"

"The more time we have, the better; three days is cutting it pretty close."

Kennan took a deep breath. "By t...t...tomorrow we've got to set this straight or announce to the media what we know. That's why they p...p...pay us the big bucks."

Acting CIA Director Schreck didn't miss the president's slurred speech and involuntary hand tremors. She shook her head and muttered silently, "Parkinson's."

...20

THE MIDDLE-AGED WOMAN"S HAND slipped between her thighs. For a few moments she moaned softly, then gasped sharply as her head rolled back on the pillow. Mossad's director of operations closed her eyes, then the hotel phone jangled.

"Everything OK?" Mossad Chief Gideon Bar-Lev asked.

"No. It's cold, rainy and *lonely* in Washington. I miss you, Gideon."

"You should have taken your husband with you—"

She broke in bluntly. "Don't go there."

"Sylvia, please do not underestimate this guy. Khalid bin Abdul Al-Aziz is a key figure in the Islamic world. His father was second in line to the Saudi throne. He's King Abdullah's nephew. The fact that *he* requested the meeting with us is important. You will need to be on your toes. No media."

Taking a deep breath, Sylvia Herzog said, "Relax. It's all arranged, my love. I'm meeting his royal-fucking-highness at the Saudi embassy at three o'clock."

Bar Lev grumbled, "Khalid is in charge of the balancing act between Riyadh and Washington. The United States buys hundreds of billions of dollars of oil, and the Saudis purchase hundreds of billions of dollars of aircraft they don't need."

Sylvia fell silent, listening.

"If you want to understand the bastard's clout, thirty-six hours after the 9-11 attack, a high-ranking CIA official—probably the director himself—phoned Khalid at his home and gave him the news. Fifteen of the nineteen hijackers were Saudis. Khalid immediately retained the services of a top public relations firm and placed newspaper ads all over the country condemning the attacks and dissociating Saudi Arabia from them. Talk about *chutzpa*: Khalid set up a hotline at the Saudi embassy in Washington for all Saudi nationals in the United States. Special travel arrangements were made, and the innocent little darlings were airlifted out of the country in spite of an FAA ban prohibiting takeoffs of all civilian aircraft regardless of destination. In spite of a total national ground-stop, Khalid had the clout to get his people out."

"You are making me nervous, darling."

"I don't want you taken in by his charm and his smooth diplomatic bullshit. Khalid requested this meeting for a reason; whatever that reason is, you can bet your sweet ass it's to benefit the House of Saud—not Israel."

"I love when you talk dirty."

THE MIDDLE-AGED WOMAN CONCEALED in a full-length burqa stepped out of a cab at the Saudi Arabian embassy on New Hampshire Avenue. A waiting embassy functionary ushered her immediately into the presence of Prince Khalid bin Aziz.

"Madam Herzog," Khalid said. "I am pleased you accepted my invitation and dressed as requested. It was kismet that you were visiting in Washington at this time."

Sylvia Herzog was a rumpled, plain-looking woman of fifty with a strong nose and piercingly intelligent eyes. She noticed that the Saudi prince blinked rarely, and then slowly, like a bird of prey. "Thank you for the invitation, Your Royal Highness." She removed her burqa and ran her fingers through her dyed-brown hair. "How your women handle these black shrouds is beyond me."

"It is an Arab tradition. As your Reb Teva was fond of saying, 'Without traditions, our lives would be as shaky as—' "

"A fiddler on the roof."

"Thank you. Actually, women wearing burqas are able to maintain a level of anonymity. In public and they are not judged on their physicality. Under the safe veil of burqas, women evade being objectified by men who might otherwise make advances or stare at their bodies."

She shrugged. "Whatever. When I put the burqa on, I told the people at the embassy that I was going to a Halloween party."

"Would you care for some Arabian coffee, or perhaps some wine? It may not be in accordance with Islamic law, but when in Rome, eh? My wine recommendation would be a Weinbach Riesling *Schlossberg Cuvee St. Catherine l'Inedit*—perhaps the finest off-dry Riesling on the planet."

Sylvia smiled. "Coffee would be lovely. I wouldn't want to return to the embassy tipsy. My next assignment would be the South Pole."

An attendant knocked. Khalid whispered instructions, and she departed silently.

Herzog glanced around. "Your Highness. Is our conversation being recorded?"

Khalid shrugged. "You have my word it is not."

She sipped her coffee. "My God, this is good."

"For a thousand years Coffee Arabia has come from mountains in Yemen. I am delighted you enjoy it." Khalid spread his hands. "It may not be chivalrous, my dear, but I too must inquire: have you any Israeli toys that transmit, record, or all of the above?"

Herzog winked and slipped off her small, silver, oval-shaped hoop earrings, handing them to the prince to examine.

He laughed mirthlessly. "You Jews are truly God's chosen entrepreneurs."

Sylvia Herzog stole a glance at her watch.

"Forgive me," Khalid said. "To the business at hand. Our two nations have at least one thing in common: a serious problem concerning Iran. Saudi Arabia cannot accept a messianic, apocalyptic Shiite cult controlling nuclear weapons. When wide-eyed believers get hold of the reins of power and weapons of mass death, we must all be seriously concerned."

Herzog made no reply.

"I trust you agree Iran is creating a sea change in the balance of power in our area. The Middle East is incendiary enough; a nuclear-arms race will make it a tinderbox."

"And you have some... ideas?"

"We admire how Israel has been able to maintain the strategic military balance—in your favor. But if Iran launches a ballistic missile with a nuclear bomb, all your F-15's cannot prevent that."

Herzog nodded pensively.

"The question then is, What will the United States do, or not do? Many Arab leaders fear that the American administration fails to understand the regional ambitions of our Persian adversary. Iran is taking advantage of President Kennan's 'reasonableness.' "

"You are preaching to the choir."

"Forgive me. I do not understand."

"It means, 'I heartily agree.' "

Khalid smiled thinly. "Recently I met with leaders of Arab countries. There was a consensus that we could not tolerate a nuclear Iran. We would support a military strike on Iran's nuclear facilities by either the U.S. or Israel. If America allows Iran to cross the nuclear threshold, the small Arab countries of the Gulf will have no choice but to leave the American orbit and ally themselves with Iran out of self-protection."

The Mossad officer remained silent.

"Trust me," Khalid added. "Small, rich, vulnerable Arab nations in the area will soon start running for cover towards Iran. They will not be brave enough to stick their finger in the big bully's eye if nobody's going to come to their support."

"Your recommendations?"

Khalid leaned forward and lowered his voice. "If your government decided to conduct a preemptive strike against Iran's main weapons and uranium-enrichment facilities with conventional aircraft..." He paused to be certain she was following his words carefully. "I am authorized to offer Saudi Arabian airspace for your pilots and ground space for refueling, and our radar will shut down for the time period required."

Sylvia Herzog silently studied the wheeler-dealer at the heart of Saudi foreign affairs. "You're serious?"

Khalid opened his desk, withdrew a document, and handed it to Herzog. It was a copy of a cable from King Abdullah, exhorting the U.S. to "cut off the head of the snake and put an end to its nuclear weapons program."

"In the wrong hands," Khalid said, "this cable would create embarrassment. I entrust it to you as a good-faith offering." He smiled, but his eyes were dark granite. "It is all true. I know you have your ways of checking. I trust that your government understands a messianic Iranian dictatorship poses not only the gravest threat to the Jewish people, but a nuclear strike against Israel doesn't serve Arab interests either."

"And therefore?" Sylvia Herzog said with a conspiratorial grin.

Prince Khalid blinked his hawk-like black eyes. "Inasmuch as the American president will never summon the political courage to attack Iran, Israel must."

...21

Tehran, Iran
November 4, 1979

THE SUN PINKED THE EASTERN SKY. Five-year-old Alie Khouri awoke to the sounds of screaming and loud popping noises outside her bedroom window. The big clock read eight o'clock. Her father rushed into her room, shaking his head in disbelief. He was winded, his soaked shirt sticking to his chest. "Hurry, dress quickly, A'isha. They are over the embassy fence. You're leaving the sandbox."

She looked out. Black smoke was rising in the distance. An over-turned car was being torched. A crowd of mostly bearded young men was shouting and swarming about the street, headed for the American Embassy. Alie was terrified. She started to cry.

Her father, Richard Khouri, had been CIA station chief in Tehran for over a quarter century. He was Muslim and one of the few in the U.S. diplomatic corps who was actually fluent in Farsi. Richard Khouri loved his assignment in Iran, the land from which his grandfather had emigrated.

"Quickly, baby. Quickly," her father said. Pausing long enough to grasp her favorite necklace, Alie followed her father. Her mother, already in the back seat, was pallid and sweaty, her thin frame racked by a cough. She grabbed Alie and held her tight. Her father had trouble maneuvering through the rampaging mob. The roar was deafening. One man on top of a car chanted through a bull-horn, "Death to America." Alie heard the crowd echo the chant.

"Why are we fleeing like common criminals?" her mother asked, pale and trembling.

THE RIYADH CONSPIRACY

"Khomeini's thugs have taken the embassy. They'll get the vaults and the files and learn that I'm CIA station head. The bastards will threaten to torture you and A'isha unless I tell them everything they want to know. I've got to get you to the airport."

Richard Khouri turned down a narrow street to avoid traffic. It was blocked. A group of masked men armed with wooden sticks and metal pipes surrounded the car. One young student poured something all over the car, then lit a match and threw it onto the gas-soaked hood.

The car was engulfed in flames. Alie heard her father calling her name. Strange hands smashed the rear window with a steel pipe, reached in and pulled the little girl to safety just before the car exploded in a ball of orange flames. Alie screamed and screamed and screamed.

...22

A'ISHA KHOURI HAD BECOME A CONNOISSEUR of death, having tasted its bitter fruits. She glanced over at her sleeping companion, thinking, *We are the same, you and I, Avram Markus, the dark side of the CIA's dark service. We are executioners, multi-linguistic assassins.*

As a matter of tradecraft, they had come to Tel Aviv, flying out of Newark on Continental Airlines rather than on the New York El Al flight tickets that Alie had purchased. Avram knew there was no such thing as too many precautions. Lulled by the drone of the jet engines, he dozed off midway through their flight.

Alie touched his shoulder, pointing to the sight of the coastal shoal of Israel unrolling like a carpet under the wing of the plane. He stretched and looked.

"That's the Jezreel Valley. I was born on kibbutz Neot Morde-chai somewhere down below." He exhaled slowly. "My family is buried there."

The plane touched down with a thump and a screech of tires. The reverse thrust screamed, the brakes jerked, and the Boeing 747-8 taxied up to the holding area. The captain, speaking in English over the intercom, ordered passengers to remain seated for security reasons.

A young Israeli security agent wearing opaque sunglasses, his shirttail hanging loose to hide the handgun tucked into his belt, strolled down the aisle checking identity photos in passports against faces. "Passports," he snapped.

Markus pulled the passport from his breast pocket and handed it over. Alie retrieved hers from her purse. The Israeli looked over the top of the passport at Markus. He compared the passport photograph to his face and smiled in apparent recognition. "Please come with me."

The security agent stepped aside so they could retrieve their carry-on luggage; then he escorted Alie and Avram down the aisle ahead of him. The other passengers gaped at the old man with a limp and the attractive young woman being hustled from the plane, trying to figure out if they were celebrities or terrorists.

Markus stepped onto the pavement outside Ben Gurion. He stood with his hands thrust deep in his pockets, shoulders stooped, feeling the familiar hot wind on his face. "Welcome to the sandbox," he said.

The sandbox. The word echoed in her brain.

"That's what old CIA field men called the Middle East."

She dug a fingernail into her palm. The last time she'd heard the expression *sandbox* was thirty years before, the day her parents were murdered in Iran.

The security agent pulled out a cell phone, switched it to camera mode, and snapped pictures of Alie and Markus. He was joined by a strikingly handsome Israeli officer with a broad natural grin, black hair, and the spare physique of a cyclist. Extending his hand, the officer said, "Remember me, Uncle Avram?"

Markus squinted, studying the intense young army captain. He shook his head. "Not little Dani. Dani Aaronson?"

The officer nodded. "Uncle Avram, you are a legend in the—"

"Don't make me sound like I'm dead," Markus interrupted. Turning to Alie, he grumbled, "Meet the nephew of Israeli's prime minister. How is Ephraim?"

"Still obstreperous. Ephraim is anxious to see you as soon as his schedule permits." A black Peugeot sedan with tinted windows pulled to the curb. Avram and Alie were assisted into the back seat, their bags placed into the trunk. Alie started to say something, but Avram cut her off with a headshake, indicating the car could be bugged.

Forty-five minutes later, the Peugeot slipped into the underground parking garage of a large drab office building overlooking King Saul Boulevard in central Tel Aviv. Favoring his game leg, Avram followed Dani Aaronson and Alie into a private elevator to the top floor. They walked past a beehive of cubicles where men and women were monitoring computers and whispering into phones. Avram eyed the dull gray painted walls. The welcome scent of fresh coffee filled his nostrils.

Sitting behind a black metal computer desk in a windowless room was a spare man dressed in khaki trousers and a white short-sleeve shirt. He had hollow cheeks, a soldier's tight haircut, thick eyebrows, and ice-cold eyes. Gideon Bar-Lev was the director general of Mossad.

"CHPINDEL GOT YOUR MESSAGE," Bar-Lev said drily. He sat in his chair, arms folded, head tilted, looking at his visitors through half-closed lids. There was a smugness about Bar-Lev that made Avram dislike him instantly.

"Coffee would be fine, thank you. This is my associate, A'isha Khouri."

Bar-Lev peered at Alie's olive skin and almond eyes. "A Muslim CIA agent?"

"Do we have an ethnicity problem?" she asked, her dark eyes flashing.

The Mossad chief shrugged. "We booked you into the Dizengoff Suites. Nearby and not too expensive." With a small, nasty smile, Bar-Lev asked, "Two rooms?"

Avram gave him a quick angry glance, nodded and remained silent.

"The only reason you're here, Markus, is that the PM requested I meet with you. Pray tell me why your CIA, with unlimited funding and thousands of active operatives, insults us by sending a washed-up deserter from the Israeli army and—" He looked again at Alie. "—his beautiful trophy Muslim—whatever?"

Bar-Lev hit an intercom button and snapped, "Coffee." Turning to Avram, he said, "The prime minister received your *urgent* message. Chpindel thinks you walk on water; you know what happened to the last guy who walked on water in the Galilee."

A knock on the door was followed by a stocky young woman carrying in two filled styrofoam cups. "Cream or sugar?" she asked.

Bar-Lev looked at Dani Aaronson. "Stop drooling over our Muslim guest. If you have time, check her into the hotel and buy her breakfast."

"Not a problem," said Captain Aaronson with a wide grin.

After they left, Bar-Lev said, "You didn't answer my question. Why *you*?"

Avram looked up from his coffee. "I don't like where this conversation is headed, Bar-Lev," he said coldly. "And I don't much like you either, but in a way you're right. I *am* burned out—and I know it." He took a deep breath, willing himself to relax.

"The CIA thinks that because I once served in the Mossad, I can waltz into your office and find out what Israel intends to do about an Iranian bomb threat." He paused. "I'm also here because my gut tells me this threat may be real. I was born on the kibbutz at Neot Mordechai. My wife, son and parents are buried there. Their friends probably still work the apple orchards and the shoe factory. One holocaust in a lifetime is enough. How could I refuse to try and stop this insanity?"

Bar-Lev reached into his top drawer and drew out a bottle. "Schnapps?" Avram shook his head.

Bar-Lev poured a short measure and downed it. "What can you Americans tell us we don't already know about a bunch of camel-fucking Iranian madmen? With our spy satellite Ofek 9, we try to keep an eye on Iran." He laughed. "We also hack into your NSA's Echelon intercepts—"

Avram cut him off. "We know the timing."

Bar-Lev raised his thick black eyebrows.

"An Iranian who worked for the Pasdaran testified that Iran was planning missile strikes against three targets: Tel Aviv, Dimona Complex, and Megiddo."

"Anybody can be paid to say anything. Did your people vet him?"

"There wasn't time. Zakariya was murdered after the video-taping."

Bar-Lev sighed in exasperation. "Keystone Cops. The way your CIA operates would be funny if it weren't so serious. You said you knew the Iranian timetable."

"The Iranian maintained that the attack would occur on 1432 on the Islamic calendar, *Eid al-Adha*, the Festival of Sacrifice. Muslims are required to make a sacrificial offering on November fifth."

The Mossad man's face blanched. "That's two days from now." He lurched to his feet, punching the intercom. "Get me Prime Minister Chpindel. Urgent."

...23

"WELCOME TO DIZENGOFF CENTER," Dani Aaronson said. "Our classic example of early ugly Israeli architecture."

Alie glanced around the neglected-looking, slightly seedy, crowded center, taking in the round pedestrian bridge with a garish rainbow-colored moving fountain in the middle. "Isn't this where the suicide attacks occurred?"

Aaronson nodded. "In 1994, and then again two years later, right where we are standing, hundreds of civilians were killed or wounded, including kids celebrating the Purim holiday." His face was pinched; his eyes narrowed. "I can understand many things about our Palestinian neighbors: their anger and disappointment and sense of injustice. All these things are human and, seen from their point of view, perhaps justifiable. What I will never understand is the pride of sending a child to destroy life, his own and others'."

Alie fell silent.

"Sorry. I'm being a terrible host. What's your pleasure: coffee, the best hummus in Israel, fast food, or a sit down restaurant with everything from Chinese to Moroccan?"

"A bathroom tops my list; then coffee."

"I'll get a table at Arcaffes." Aaronson felt his heart pound, following Alie with his eyes. He picked an outside table, ordered black coffee, and hit a preprogrammed button on his cell phone. "Anything doing?"

"The colonel is looking for you. Another night-training exercise. Seven p.m."

"Shit. I had other plans tonight," he muttered, unaware of Alie's silent arrival.

"Problem?" she asked.

"My unit's conducting an exercise tonight. I had hoped to show you Tel Aviv."

She ignored the invitation. "What unit do you serve with, Captain?"

"Shayetet 13."

Alie arched her eyebrows, scrutinizing him. "I'm impressed. You're a Badass?"

Aaronson looked confused.

"The CIA classified the world's nine elite special forces and named them Badasses: Russia's Spetsnaz, of course; the French Naval Commandos, the *beret verts*; MARSOC, the U.S. Marine group; U.S. Army Rangers and Green Berets; the British SAS—Special Air Service; plus U. S. Navy SEALs and your Shayetet 13."

Aaronson shrugged. "We specialize in sea-to-land incursions, maritime hostage rescue; all that good stuff." He grinned. "Our motto is, 'When the going gets tough, the Jews get pissed.' Now it's my turn: a Muslim *and* a CIA operative. Isn't that unusual?"

"I am a Muslim, but I despise the people behind 9-11. They twisted the concept of *jihad* into something ugly and indefensible. After those planes hit the buildings, there was a ramp-up at the CIA, a rush to hire college graduates fluent in Arabic. I graduated on a scholarship from the University of Michigan. I loved sports, but the only sport for women was basketball, and as you can see, I am not tall enough." She paused to sip her coffee. "Detroit and Dearborn were rough areas. I took up *Capoeira*."

He wrinkled his forehead. "You took up what?"

"*Capoeira* is a four-hundred-year-old Brazilian martial art originated by African slaves to protect themselves. In Brazil, practitioners were forced to practice in secret, because it can be deadly. The highest belt is the coveted red rope."

"And of course you have—"

She nodded. He raised both hands in surrender.

Alie paused several seconds. "My father worked for the CIA. I knew he would have wanted me to serve the country he loved. I'm fluent in Arabic, in good shape, unmarried—the perfect CIA candidate. Right?" She smiled and squeezed his arm. "When we arrived, you called Avram Markus a legend."

"My uncle said Avram could have been our next Moishe Dayan. He was brilliant, his troops loved him, and he was one of only forty Israelis ever to be awarded the Medal of Valor. It's a damn shame."

"What happened?"

"According to what I've heard, Avram met an exquisitely beautiful Druid Muslim girl from a border village near his kibbutz in the Jezreel Valley. They fell in love. She was seventeen; he was twenty. She was going to the Rafic Hariri School of Nursing in Beirut. He was in the army. They didn't involve friends or family with what they had between them. Their friends wouldn't have understood, and getting their families together was impossible to imagine. But you know Avram when he makes his mind up. They married, lived on the kibbutz Neot Mordechai, and had a baby boy." Dani signaled for two coffee refills.

"It was tragic. One day his wife was visiting her family in the town of Ghajar. The baby was with her. A few miles to the north, Hezbollah had ambushed an IDF patrol, killing three Israeli soldiers; they were firing rockets from positions north of Ghajar. In trying to target the source of the rocket launchers, Israeli artillery fired several short rounds that accidentally struck the town of Ghajar. Avram's wife and son were killed."

She felt the color drain from her face. "Friendly fire?"

"More like damned unfriendly fire. Avram was teaching a Mossad class. My uncle was Avram's superior officer in the army. He went with Prime Minister Shamir to break the news. Shamir was having political problems at the time. He feared if news of the army's ineptness hit the papers, his government might not hold together. Shamir enforced a news blackout and ordered Avram to remain silent about the incident."

Dani laughed. "Ephraim said Avram told the prime minister to go fuck himself. He left the next morning for the United States. Your CIA chief was more than happy to pick up Mossad's top operative, the legendary Scorpion."

Alie found herself staring at Dani. He was an incredibly attractive young man with a long straight nose and deep blue eyes turned down at the corners, the smile careful but confident. Several times she had to restrain herself from reaching out and touching his sensuous lips. She thought, *I would love to get this young Greek god into my bed... and into my body... and into my life. But first things first.*

As if reading her mind, Dani Aaronson asked, "Let me walk you to the hotel."

"Thank you, Captain, but I would love to shop a bit."

"Please call me Dani. Are you free for dinner one evening?"

She touched his arm again lightly. "Sounds wonderful. I would love to see you again, Dani, and to meet your Uncle Ephraim. My assignment is to escort Avram Markus, but I don't know his schedule. If I have free time, can I call you?"

Dani handed her a card. "Call any time, night or day." He winked. "Night is better." He kissed her on the cheek, waved and strode off.

Alie depressed the number on her phone. When it was answered, she said, "All systems are go." Then she rang off.

...24

THE MOSSAD CHIEF'S BULLETPROOF AUDI A8L barreled along Route 2. Gideon Bar-Lev was driving; he turned off at the Caesarea interchange. Avram, exhausted from jet lag, napped in the back seat, too tired to care.

"Ephraim's not well; we're meeting at his home," Bar-Lev said. "Rubin and Agus will be there. They served with Chpindel in the Army. Rubin is the highest intelligence officer in the IDF; Agus is head of Shin Bet. We three are the co-equal heads of the Israeli intelligence community."

Through half-closed eyelids Avram watched the greenish-blue haze hovering over the Mediterranean shoreline. He dozed as they passed Caesarea's ancient Roman ruins, barely noticing the white sandy beach at Sdot-Yam. He pressed his thumb and forefinger to the bridge of his nose and tried to rub away the fatigue.

Bar-Lev continued. "Natasha Schleider will be there; she's deputy prime minister and leader of the right wing Yisrael Beiteinu party." He gave an exasperated sigh. "Schleider can be a real bitch; her dream is to replace Chpindel as prime minister."

Bar-Lev eased the Audi into a gravel courtyard shaded by umbrella pines fronting a honey-colored villa. Avram inhaled the familiar scent of the eucalyptus trees bordering the courtyard. Hard-eyed, well-armed security agents chatted lazily in the patches of brilliant sunshine.

The dining room shades were down, the room cool and in semi-darkness. Avram was distracted at the sight of his old boss. The years had not been kind to Ephraim Chpindel. His once black hair was now thin and peppered with white; his lean soldier's body had gone heavy; his hands were cord-veined and liver-spotted.

The prime minister caught his glance and nodded. "I'm old. But not dead yet."

Markus didn't hear the words. He felt his eyes sting. The last time Avram had seen Chpindel seemed a lifetime ago, a moment seared into his memory.

"OLD, BUT NOT DEAD YET," Chpindel repeated, forcing Avram back to the present. A facial droop caused Chpindel's lips to pull a little to one side.

"I didn't know you were ill."

"Advertising it would have only worried my friends and made the Arabs happy." Chpindel smiled a lopsided smile and shrugged.

Markus heard car doors slamming. Two somber-faced men entered. He presumed the tall, burly, square-chested man with close-cropped hair was Rubin, the head of Aman. Avram was surprised by the other man's unimpressive physical stature: short, wiry, his deep-set brown eyes lending his face an air of profound intelligence.

"Avram Markus," Chpindel said. "Meet Uri Rubin and Ya'akov Agus."

"Markus," Rubin echoed. "Your name sounds familiar." He snapped his fingers. "You were part of the Wrath of God Operation—"

The prime minister broke in. "After the PLO murdered our eleven athletes at the Munich Olympics, Golda Meir unofficially authorized Mossad to target anyone who had participated in or abetted the massacre. We intended to draw the world's attention to what happens to those who kill Israelis. And thanks in part to Avram's help, we did."

There was a hiss of indignation at the doorway.

"Is this a Sayeret Matkal reunion?" Natasha Schleider grumbled.

Chpindel exhaled heavily. "It's nice to see you, Natasha." The prime minister and the deputy premier had dropped any pretense of liking each other. Her bullish attitude and uncompromising right-wing positions nettled Chpindel. They were adversaries; everyone in the room knew it.

To Avram he said, "Natasha came to Israel from Russia at age thirty and missed mandatory military service in the IDF. Her friendly style comes from feeling like an outsider, not having had the privilege of dying for Israel."

"Nonsense," said Schleider, shaking hands with Avram. She was a solid woman with broad shoulders and black hair. Her eyes were intense, her grip a vise.

After everyone was seated at the dining room table, Chpindel said, "I invited Avram Markus to join us. He served with distinction in the Sayeret Matkal and then in Mossad until an unfortunate incident forced him to leave Israel and work for the CIA. He brings us highly classified information from the American government. I needn't remind everyone that this meeting is secret." He glared at Schleider. "No leaks to DEBKAfile or the *Jerusalem Post*. Understand? We can't have our people in a panic."

"So tell us already," Schleider barked. "What's going on?"

Chpindel motioned to Bar-Lev, who cleared his throat. "We know that Iran has cloned versions of the Chinese M-9 and M-11 SRBMs. The M-9 has a range of 600 kilometers and is equipped with a single nuclear warhead. The M-11 has a range of 400 kilometers and carries an 800 kilogram warhead—"

"Eight hundred kilograms," interrupted Ya'akov Agus. "That's 16 kilotons—the size bomb the Americans dropped on Hiroshima."

Bar-Lev spoke again. "We knew from agents in place that the M-9 had been successfully test fired." He looked at Avram. "According to Markus, the American CIA interrogated an Iranian Revolutionary Guard informer. The man confirmed the Iranian missiles are operational."

"That's not proof," said Agus.

"The Iranian informer was assassinated in London the night of the taping."

The people at the table exchanged worried looks.

Bar-Lev referred to his notes. "Having launch capability is one thing; having payloads to mount on their missiles is another." He paused. "What's worrisome is our assets in Jordan are reporting rumors of an impending Iranian attack using nuclear warheads. Where the Iranians sourced these warheads, we don't know. The Saudis are passing similar information to people who they know will get word to us."

"The Saudis?" Chpindel asked.

Bar-Lev nodded. "With the Saudis, you never know. They are active at every level of the terror chain, from planners to financiers. But Saudi intelligence did provide warnings to the Americans about the bombs shipped by FedEx and UPS from Yemen. They may be telling the truth this time. Mossad's concern has been, Does Iran really have the bombs, and if so, are they insane enough to use them against us, knowing our counter-strike capability? I asked for this meeting because the Americans believe Iran not only has nuclear bombs, but is actually planning to launch them—within days."

Chpindel's dining room was hushed. All eyes were on Markus.

"Yesterday, I met former KGB General Pyotr Sergeyevich Zhukov in New York. Zhukov is a high-up in the Russian Mafia in America; he is also well connected in Russia. Over the years, we did favors for each other. Zhukov was commander of the 13th GUMO in the city of Ozerrzk. His troops protected the largest nuclear weapons storage facility in Russia. Zhukov told me bombs were stored in warehouses protected only by cheap padlocks and guards who more often than not didn't show up.

"Zhukov had a half dozen vodkas. He gave me information. It could have been the vodka talking, it could have been planted misinformation, or it could be the truth. I don't know. He said an unknown number of bombs had disappeared from inventory.

"I asked if any of these missing bombs could have been shipped to the Middle East. He appeared to be drunk, but Zhukov is an old fox. He said these exact words: 'Tell your overrated ex-employer, the Mossad, to check shipments from Kaliningrad destined for Algeria or some other phony destination.' "

Chpindel turned to his military chief of staff. "Uri, has Ofed-9 picked up any unusual activity at the Iranian missile sites?"

Rubin shook his head. "We operate multiple satellites in space: Ofed-5 and 7; ImageSat's EROS-A and EROS-B1, and TechSAR. Each satellite completes an orbit every ninety minutes. There is no unusual activity reported at the Iranian missile sites—"

Schleider broke in. "They could launch missiles from anywhere. Iran's a country with 600,000 square miles."

"Unfortunately, you're right, Natasha," Bar-Lev admitted. "The M-11 is a mobile launcher which could be camouflaged and not picked up by our satellites."

"We will do our best," General Rubin said calmly.

Chpindel picked up the phone. "Get me Meir Rivkin."

Over the speakerphone, the head of the signal intelligence arm of the Israeli Defense Force answered in a curt tone. "Rivkin here."

"This is Ephraim Chpindel."

"I recognized your voice."

"Your Stuxnet virus proved a great success—"

"What do you need this time, Mr. Prime Minister?"

"Arrogant bastard," Rubin whispered to Avram. "But the man's a bloody genius."

Chpindel fired back, "I have an *urgent* assignment, Meir."

Everyone heard a deep sigh over the speakerphone.

"I'm sending someone to see you. He will be there within the hour and explain what we need. Unit 8200 is in total lockdown mode until the mission is complete."

Turning to Avram, he said, "You know what to tell Rivkin."

Chpindel began to cough, a violent cough that shook his body. His usually calm gray eyes looked anxious. "The old days were hard times." With a weary sigh, he added, "Always, we have hard times, eh?"

...25

AVRAM WAS DROPPED OFF in the Negev Desert nineteen miles west of Beersheba at Urim SIGINT, the signal intelligence-gathering installation operated by Unit 8200. He looked up at the mesh of aerials, microwave dishes and satellite communication transmitters pointed skyward from the Israeli Defense Force facility.

He was directed to the small office of Meir Rivkin, the head of Urim SIGINT. Rivkin was an obese, unshaven man with hooded eyes and an oversized head. The young man's fingers flew over his computer keyboard. Thick cigarette smoke hung in the air. "Be with you in a sec."

Avram glanced out of Rivkin's cubicle into a brightly lit area lined with row upon row of computer workstations manned by shockingly young-looking technicians. He was beginning to feel shaky and his head ached. It had been hours since he had eaten. "How about coffee?"

Rivkin nodded absently. He took a long pull from his cigarette, peering at the screen. "I'm impressed," he mumbled. "Served in Sayeret Matkal; holder of the Medal of Valor." His eyes remained fixed on the computer. "Mossad picked you up in '74."

"I thought Mossad information was highly classified."

The signal intelligence head tapped cigarette ash on the floor, chuckled and patted the screen. "There is nothing on computers that can't be recaptured—if you have the right brains and equipment." He turned back to the green tube. "You're credited with killing two member of the Black September group in '73: Hussein al Bashir in Nicosia and Zaiad Muchasi in his Athens hotel room—with a bomb. Cool."

Avram leaned over the desk, grabbing Rivkin tightly by his collar. Rivkin's face flushed deep red; he coughed. Avram growled, "I didn't travel six thousand miles to listen to a eulogy. You may be a computer prima donna to Chpindel, but not to me. Time is short. You do what needs to be done or—" Avram extended his forefinger like a pointed gun, lifted it to his lips, blew imaginary smoke and winked. "And I want coffee. Now."

RIVKIN'S TWO SECTION HEADS settled into cracked black vinyl folding chairs drawn up to a metal conference table. Meir Rivkin sat at the head with Avram immediately to his right. Esther Winer sat on one side of the table; Moshe Kasoff sat on the other. Everyone except Avram had a laptop computer perched on the table.

"Chpindel sent this guy to brief us," Rivkin said. "I looked him up. Markus was an Israeli war hero—before we were born."

No one laughed.

Avram took a breath before he spoke. "We have a reliable rumor—"

"A reliable rumor is an oxymoron," Moshe Kasoff broke in, chuckling.

Avron fixed Kasoff with a hard stare. "If an Iranian M-11 missile drops a 20 kiloton warhead on Tel Aviv three days from now—a bomb larger than the one dropped on Hiroshima—would that strike you as funny as well?"

Kasoff looked deflated. "I was just—"

Esther Winer said irritably, "Mr. Markus, young computer people like Moshe tend to be irreverent; they are also brilliant, and irreplaceable. If the clock is ticking, don't waste time lecturing us. How can we help?"

Avram grunted and nodded. "Iran has attained missile launch capacity up to a range of six hundred kilometers. We have unconfirmed information of an imminent attack, the target areas being

Megiddo, Tel Aviv and the Dimona Complex here in the Negev. Chpindel and his people have to make a crucial decision—whether or not to launch a preemptive strike. The key question is, do they actually have nuclear warheads? I received information from a former Russian general that a half-dozen bombs in the 10 to 20 kiloton range were sold to Iran and recently shipped from Kaliningrad."

Rivkin asked, "To what destination port?"

"Don't know. Maybe Algeria. The manifest would be falsified."

Esther Winer said, "A ship could list any Arab nation as a destination and still go to Iran. Do you know the shipping company or vessel name?"

Markus shrugged, shaking his head. "I'm sorry. That's all the information we have. Chpindel needs your group to locate and identify the ship, determine its destination port and estimated arrival time—and we need to know yesterday."

Meir Rivkin stood up. "Kasoff, get your team members to burrow into computers of all shipping companies using the Port of Kaliningrad. Esther, you track all vessels departing for anywhere near Iran in the last two to four weeks. Hack out their manifests. Before we can ask for satellite pictures, we need to know everything about the vessel. Get on it. I'll check with you both later."

Rivkin's phone buzzed. He turned to Avram. "The prime minister is tied up with a meeting tonight with his advisers. He wants you to come in the morning instead."

Esther Winer's soft brown eyes widened behind her black-rimmed glasses. She gave Avram a furtive look. "I live just off highway 40 south of Tel Aviv. When was the last time you had a home-cooked meal?"

...26

THE PRIME MINISTER'S FACE WAS A MASK, betraying nothing. He was a thoughtful man, not known to be ruled by emotions. Chpindel glanced around the room, making eye contact with Rubin, Agus and Schleider. "As you all know, I am on record in opposition to setting loose the 'dogs of war' in lieu of negotiations."

Natasha Schleider exhaled in frustration. "We have a right to defend ourselves."

Chpindel cut her off. "Natasha, allow me to finish. It would be naive not to acknowledge the harsh reality of this situation. Iran's religious zealots possess the means, motive and opportunity to do us irreparable harm. Tehran has a cache of advanced missiles capable of delivering nuclear warheads to targets anywhere in Israel."

Schleider said, "Every time that maniac Hanoush appears on Iranian television, he expresses his intention to see Israel consumed by a nuclear fireball."

"What you say is true, Natasha. I am not blind to the crucial lesson of history: bad things get worse if they're not challenged early. The world conveniently forgets two out of every three Jews were murdered in Hitler's Europe."

Chpindel took a labored breath. "Whether Hanoush is a religious fanatic, a lunatic or a shrewd politician, we don't know. It is possible Iran's reform-minded Green Movement will somehow replace the mullah-led regime, or at least temper their ideological extremism. At this moment, there is simply not enough hard evidence to authorize a preemptive attack." He sighed deeply and paused to drink a glass of water.

Schleider turned to General Rubin. "If Hanoush delivered on his promise, how much time would we have from launch to impact?"

"A couple of minutes. Perhaps enough time to initiate counter-strikes. But that isn't the key point. We would not be able to stop the destruction."

Natasha Schleider stared at the prime minister in stony silence, her chin at a defiant angle. "Ephraim, we stand alone, except for those Christians who support Israel so they can have their 'Rapture,' fly to heaven and meet their Christ. And, of course, the New York Jews, who give us advice from the safety of gated communities. We can't count on the Americans to do anything but wring hands and take up television collections for survivors. Their politicians have no stomach and no money for overseas adventures after Iraq and Afghanistan. American warships are here, but I don't know what assistance they could provide, except psychological. We Jews are a nervous people. Nineteen centuries of Christian and Muslim love have taken a toll."

"If I may be permitted a word," said Ya'akov Agus. "I realize the threat we face is potentially catastrophic. Until we know for certain that Iran has operational nuclear warheads to load on to their missiles, I oppose unilateral action. A preemptive attack will rupture our tenuous relations with Washington; we would solidify the rule of the mullahs in Tehran; we would cause the price of oil to spike to cataclysmic highs and place communities across the Jewish Diaspora in danger. We will also accelerate Israel's conversion from a once-admired refuge for a persecuted people into a leper among nations—"

Rubin interrupted. His voice was firm, commanding. The general was accustomed to making life and death decisions. "I know ordering a preemptive strike is a difficult decision; we do not have the luxury or trauma of hindsight knowing what would have happened if we failed to act. Most Arab leaders will applaud us silently; the West will criticize us, but we might be saving six million Jewish lives. Therefore, I reluctantly agree with Natasha. Action is required. American warships cannot be counted on. Their Navy has no defense for the Russian SS-N-22 Sunburn anti-ship cruise missiles. It is the most lethal missile in the world today, and Iran has it."

"You underestimate the Americans if you think they are dumb enough to put five carriers in the Gulf," Chpindel said. "They will move their Marine and Navy air units to Qatar, the UAE, or Bahrain, depending on the political climate there."

Rubin shook his head. "Remember in the Falklands War when the French-made Exocet missiles, fired from Argentine fighters, sunk the *HMS Sheffield*? And in 1987, during the Iran-Iraq war, the American ship *USS Stark* was cut in half by a pair of Exocets in the Persian Gulf. Ephraim, I'm sorry to tell you, but the Sunburn is larger than the Exocet, has a greater range and a superior guidance system. The Sunburn missile was specifically designed by the Russians to defeat the U.S. Aegis radar defense system. The Americans know it. I told Admiral Baysinger personally the last time I was in Washington."

Chpindel asked, "Are you forgetting the American AWACs radar planes that stay aloft on a rotating schedule? Can't the AWACs detect everything threatening to the American fleet, and aren't they augmented with intelligence from orbiting satellites?"

Rubin grimaced. "If it wasn't the Persian Gulf, you would be right. Iran's rugged northern shore offers concealment of mobile missile launchers; detection is problematic. The U.S. Navy has never faced anything as formidable as the Sunburn missile."

Chpindel felt a sudden weight of depression pushing down against his shoulders. The strain was causing his words to slur. "I still find it difficult to believe Iran would launch a nuclear warhead at Tel Aviv or anywhere else. They know we have a destructive reprisal capability. They know that they would be putting the Persian civilization at risk."

Uri Rubin put his hand on Chpindel's shoulder. "Get some rest, Ephraim. We need you at the helm. We can reassemble when you're feeling better."

Chpindel nodded, his forehead glistening with sweat.

Natasha Schleider crashed her fist on the table. "As it says in Job: 'They that plow iniquity and sow mischief shall reap the same.' The Arabs believe they are winning because we withdrew unilaterally from Gaza; they tell their masses Hamas defeated us. They blew up 241 U.S. Marines in Beirut in 1983, and the Iranian regime paid no price—in fact, Reagan withdrew his troops. They paid no price for the two attacks in Argentina against the Jewish embassy and the Jewish center, nor for killing the U.S. servicemen in the Khobar Towers bombing in Saudi Arabia in 1996."

As the child of Russian parents who had survived the horrors of the Dachau death camp, she was bitter. "Ben Gurion warned us. 'As long as the Arabs think they can destroy the Jewish state, there will be no peace.' We must make them understand once and for all that if they raise their hands against us, we'll put them back in the Stone Age." She glared at Ephraim Chpindel. "Mr. Prime Minister, if you are unwilling or incapable of doing what is necessary to protect Israel—I am."

"MS. KHOURI'S ROOM," Avram told the hotel operator. When the phone was answered he said, "Hello, it's me. I'm tied up tonight. Can you manage by yourself?"

"Of course. I'll wash my hair, have a soak and order room service." There was a short pause. "Are you meeting with your friend, the prime minister?"

"No, tomorrow morning."

"Shall I accompany you? That's what I'm being paid for, you know."

"Let's touch base in the morning." He hung up.

From memory, Alie punched in a number. "I'll be needing the package we discussed." She glanced at her watch: 4 p.m. "Meet me in one hour on the northeast corner of Gordon and Dizongoff Street."

TRAFFIC ON HIGHWAY 40 WAS HEAVY. Avram glanced at Esther Winer, who was driving. The woman was in her late fifties with thick, black, unstyled hair and pale brown eyes that shone with a calm intelligence.

"I overheard Ephraim Chpindel complimenting Rivkin about the Stuxnet virus."

Esther rolled her eyes upward in exasperation. "Meir Rivkin *is* a cyber genius; he is also ambitious and likes to hog the credit. Meir is angling for a promotion to Unit 8200 headquarters in Glilot Junction."

Avram persisted. "The Stuxnet virus served what purpose?"

"Iran's nuclear centrifuges, including those at the Natanz and Bushehr reactors, were infected with a worm, a virus that causes significant delays in their nuclear project." She looked across and smiled. "The Stuxnet cybercode contained the word *myrtus*. That's Latin for myrtle tree. Do you remember your Hebrew?"

"Myrtle means Hadassah, which translated is Esther." Avram looked confused. "You're the one who created the Stuxnet virus?"

Esther gave an exasperated sigh. "Yes. And goodhearted Rivkin gave me a bottle of Metaxa and a fancy new cell phone instead of a raise. I developed a sophisticated piece of software—a malicious little worm. When the virus worm gets introduced into the Iranian centrifuges, it infects everything. The worm has two major components. One was designed to send their nuclear centrifuges out of control." She grinned. "The other computer program secretly recorded what normal operations at the nuclear plant looked like, then played these readings back to plant operators like a pre-recorded security tape at a bank robbery, so that it appeared everything was operating normally while the centrifuges were actually tearing themselves apart."

"How long did it take you?"

"About two years. The reason Stuxnet was so effective is that we tested it out carefully. Behind the barbed wire that you saw, we created nuclear centrifuges virtually identical to Iran's at Natanz, where they are struggling to enrich uranium."

"How were you able to inject the virus into Iranian computers?"

"The Iranian nuclear program's computers are not connected to the Internet, so I couldn't introduce the virus online. We had contacts with a Russian firm helping to build the Bushehr nuclear power plant. We arranged to scatter infected USB sticks near the Russians' computers. Chances were better than fifty-fifty that human nature would cause someone to pick one up and insert it in their computer."

"Stuxnet delayed the Iranians capability to enrich uranium, right?"

"Yes."

"For how long?"

She shrugged. "There is no guarantee the attacks were not fully successful. Some parts of Iran's operations ground to a halt, while others may have survived, according to the reports of international nuclear inspectors. We believe we crippled Iran's capability for a year or two without triggering a war that might have followed an overt military strike of the kind we conducted against Iraq in 1981."

"If Iran was preparing a strike, they would have imported nuclear warheads for their missiles," he mused out loud, trying to shake off grim forebodings. He forced a smile. "Congratulations on Stuxnet. You are older than the others in Rivkin's group."

She flashed a flirtatious smile. "Older, but more experienced."

"Married?"

Her shoulders sagged. "Before the War in Lebanon in 2006, my husband Shaul was a professor of computer science at the Weisman Institute. I was a computer geek—a systems security specialist working for RSA Security. Shaul was offered a job in America at Princeton as department chair of computer science. We planned to wait until our son, Alon, finished his three years of compulsory military service." Esther's voice trailed off.

Avram noticed she wedged the knuckle of her right forefinger between her teeth. He said nothing. Experience had taught him to be patient.

"In July 2006, Hezbollah militants ambushed two Israeli Humvees patrolling our side of the border fence. They killed three IDF soldiers. Two others were taken prisoner." She inhaled deeply. "My son was killed in a failed rescue attempt."

Her face turned ashen. "The loss of Alon put a heavy strain on my life and on our marriage. With the death of a child, some couples turn to each other. Some turn on each other." She sighed. "Shaul wasn't there for me and didn't want anyone to be there for him. He took the job at Princeton. I volunteered for the Israeli Intelligence Corps and was assigned to Urim SIGINT. We live apart."

Avram nodded grimly. They drove on in silence. Shortly after sunset, he gazed at the glimmering lights of Tel Aviv on the horizon

117

ahead. He felt his heart pounding. "I also lost my son," he whispered in a low voice, "and my wife—a long time ago."

Then he told Esther the whole story.

"GLASSES ARE IN THE SIDEBOARD; the Metaxa bottle is around somewhere. See if you can find it while I fix dinner. Do you like taboule?"

Avram smiled as he opened the Greek brandy and poured. "The last time I had taboule was at my kibbutz, Neot Mordechai." They clinked glasses. "*L'chaim*."

He stood by the sink watching Esther rinse parsley and set bulgur wheat in a bowl. "Metaxa is strong stuff," he cautioned. "We better go easy." While Esther waited for the bulgur to soak, she took out tomatoes, scallions, garlic, lemon juice and olive oil. "Do you prefer taboule on pita or as a salad?" Esther asked. Her new cell phone chirped, and she answered. "It's Rivkin, for you. He sounds excited." She handed Avram the phone.

"Markus, we located the ship, the *Samaria*, a 4,000-ton, 98-meter general cargo vessel. It set sail from Pietarsaari, Finland, for the Port of Bushehr, Iran. The vessel is manned by fifteen Russian nationals and is owned by a multi-layered syndicate named *Suedasso* out of Panama. It sails under the Maltese flag and is carrying roughly $1.85 million worth of timber."

Rivkin paused to catch his breath. "You were right. Prior to leaving for Finland, the *Samaria* underwent unspecified repairs at the Russian enclave on the Baltic Sea, Kaliningrad. On the manifest it lists five gas-powered water pumps loaded on board in Kaliningrad."

"Have you contacted Chpindel?"

"Of course."

"When is the ship scheduled to arrive in Bushehr?"

"That's the rub. The *Samaria* was due in port yesterday. We're too late."

"Meir, the real world is not as predictable as your cyber world. Contact Rubin for satellite photos of the Bushehr port area. When I flew in two days ago, the Channel and French coast were experiencing thunderstorms and turbulence. Bad weather may delay the ship's arrival. You need up-to-date satellite pictures. And you need them now."

"Bad news?" Esther asked as she put the food on the table.

"The Russian ship may have already unloaded in Iran. Nuclear warheads could be anywhere in Iran. Rivkin took away my appetite."

"Have more Metaxa," Esther coaxed. "There is nothing else for you to do."

Avram raised the refilled glass up to the light, sloshing it slightly, studying the refracted rays passing through the brandy. Thinking. He lowered the glass instead of drinking from it. "If Iran launches a strike," he said quietly, "their leaders will, of course, know about it. And they will also expect we will immediately launch a counter-strike. So what will they be doing now?"

Esther answered, "Moving their families out of harm's way."

"Right, and transferring funds out of the country. Let's go to your computer."

Seated behind the green glow of her console, Esther said, "Okay."

"Print out a list of Iran's civilian and military leadership."

Esther's fingers darted across the keyboard. She clicked her mouse and keyed in *print*. The printer rumbled; a sheet of paper slithered out.

Avram studied the list, marking off a dozen names. "I want to know about these guys: the director of Iran's Atomic Energy Agency; the minister of foreign affairs; the head of Iran's Intelligence and Security Agency; the chief of the army, and naturally, the leader of the Revolution's Guards. Don't worry about President Hanoush. He's a religious fanatic; he wouldn't leave Tehran. Tap into their home phones, cell phones, pagers, faxes, and e-mails. Then check bank accounts; any large sums transferred; trips planned. Look for anything unusual."

Esther nodded.

"How long for results?"

"A few hours."

"So fast?" Avram looked encouraged.

"Traditional search engines require a full day to crawl across the entire online universe. This one isn't kosher, but it's fast. It's a program that enlists other search engines to do our work. This way we harness the power of a multitude of engines." She finished preparing her search program and typed in the names Avram had selected.

"Here we go," Esther said, launching the program. At blinding speed the five Iranian's names were being compared to data all over the world, looking for match-ups.

"Now we wait."

Avram stood close, peering at the computer screen.

She stretched, complaining, "My shoulders are stiff."

He gently massaged her tight shoulder muscles. "Oh my God, that feels so good." Esther's breath quickened. She pivoted around in her chair and faced Avram. "I believe that I can do with another hit of Metaxa."

"Metaxa has a high alcohol content."

She took a large swig. "You are welcome to stay here tonight," Esther said huskily. "I can drive you to Chpindel's in the morning."

Before he could respond, she added with a twinkle, "When we get the computer results, you will be here to evaluate them." As he stood behind her, she reached back and rubbed his thigh. A heavy silence settled between them.

Esther finished off her glass. "Would it embarrass you to hear that middle-aged women are more sexually active and enjoy better orgasms than younger women?"

Avram reddened.

Esther's eyebrows arched. "Or perhaps Israel's Medal of Valor hero is getting old, and perhaps the eternal masculine craving for female flesh has finally left him in peace?"

He slowly shook his head. The furtive glances, the comments made only half in jest, the warm, humid air, the Metaxa all coalesced to create sexual tension.

"Are you familiar with the *Tehumin*?" Esther asked. Without waiting for his answer, she said, "The *Tehumin* is the journal of the Zomet Institute, which applies Jewish law to such modern-day issues as technology, medicine, politics and security."

Avram looked puzzled, but he remained silent.

She winked. "Sex is permissible where national security is concerned. The *Tehumin* cites as precedent my namesake, Queen Esther, who screwed the Persian King Ahasuerus and saved the Jewish people from genocide." She moved her hand from his thigh to between his legs and squeezed gently. "Wouldn't you say what we are doing tonight is in Israel's national interest?"

Avram touched her forehead softly and then answered her with a kiss. Her lips were soft and moist. A few minutes later her hands were inside his clothes and his inside hers. She felt him hardening against her, felt herself softening against him, felt ready to give herself to him standing up, like a couple of teenagers.

SOMETIME AFTER MIDNIGHT AVRAM STIRRED and checked his watch: 1 a.m. He lay still for a long moment, listening to her soft snoring. He hadn't felt this peaceful in years, though guilt was hovering in the recesses of his conscience. Esther sensed his movement, clicked on the light and crawled out of bed. "I'll check the computer. Be right back."

She returned, frowning. "Either I screwed up royally," she said, "or nothing—and I mean nothing—out of the ordinary is going on in Tehran. No unexplained increases in bank balances. No sudden trips to faraway places. No untraceable phone calls. Nothing suspicious. Home phone intercepts were unremarkable, except for teen-age girls gossiping about boys. No mention of the *Samaria* or hints of imminent military activity. I even checked the military barracks at Bushehr. No special orders or alerts. I'm confused."

He sat on the edge of the bed in his shorts. "If Iran was planning on bombing Israel, they would expect a retaliatory strike. Certainly the troops at Bushehr would be on highest alert. All of this inactivity couldn't be staged."

"Could Iran be using the Hezbollah in Lebanon to launch their attack?"

"Anything is possible. Even with surrogates, Iran would expect to pay a price."

She whispered, "In times like this, I turn to religion. Are you familiar with Psalm 23:4?" Without waiting for his answer, Esther turned off the light, slipped her hand inside his shorts, squeezed and said, " 'Even though I walk through the valley of the shadow of death, thy rod and whatever, they comfort me.' "

...28

IT WAS NOON WHEN THEY ENTERED CAESERIA. Esther pulled to the side of the road. She handed Avram a slip of paper. It had nothing on it but a telephone number. She also gave him an odd-shaped electronic unit. "This is Rivkin's gift to me, a 6GS cell phone with an untappable channel." She smiled warmly and squeezed his arm. "Call me."

AVRAM SAID TO CHPINDEL, "When all this Iranian mess is over—"

"I'm afraid *all this* will never be over," Chpindel cut in. "Netanyahu said, 'If the Arabs put down their weapons today, there would be no more violence. If the Jews put down their weapons today, there would be no more Israel.' I'm afraid he was right."

"I live in Florida," Avram said. "One day I saw a cute girl wearing a tight tee shirt that read, 'Violence is never the answer, but sometimes, like with cockroaches, it is the only possible response.' She may have been right also."

Chpindel sighed. "I remember when you told me violence was a last resort."

"Over many years it became a last resort more often than I would have preferred."

The prime minister nodded thoughtfully. The windows were open, and a light breeze stirred the humid air through the curtains.

"Your nephew Dani greeted me at the airport. He is a personable young man."

"Dani is the son I never had. He is a member of Shayetet 13. After his service, Dani has a future with the Office, if he wants it.

Gideon Bar-Lev has no social smarts; rubs too many people the wrong way. It's time for lunch. Are you hungry?"

"Starved."

"Come. Sit. Sarah," he called out, "we're ready."

The iron-willed nurse who ran the household carried in two plates. "Please try and eat something, Ephraim."

"I don't have much appetite, but I do like a little pork loin now and then."

"Pork? The Israeli prime minister eats pork?"

"It's a state secret, punishable by death. If the knitted yarmulkes found out, I would lose the backing of the religious ideologues. We would have new elections."

"Is that your fatalistic Israeli sense of humor?"

Chpindel took a sip of coffee, his cup shaking slightly. "You need a sense of humor these days." He stopped talking and looked at his old friend with one eyebrow raised. "Tell me, what is your opinion of this Iranian mess?"

"I ask myself, Who benefits if the Jewish State of Israel and the leading Shiite Muslim nation in the Middle East severely cripple each other?"

The prime minister gave a stoic nod of his head and continued eating.

Avram held up three fingers. "In my experience there are three types of evil-doers: the revenge seekers, the religious fanatics, and the strategic plotters." He smiled. "Let's examine the evil-doer candidates: Russia, Iran, Saudi Arabia and China. Who benefits the most?"

Greeted by continued silence, he answered his own question. "Given the present circumstances, Iran would top the list. The present Iranian government is run by fanatical clerics. It is also true that Iran continues to fund and assist Hamas, Hezbollah, Islamic Jihad, and whoever else they want, while advancing the one goal that unites every one of these groups: the eradication of Israel."

Chpindel nodded slowly. "Parvis Hanoush is a firm believer in the apocalyptic end times as stated in the Koran. He's got one hand on the Koran and the other on the trigger. Hanoush understands Shiites make up fifteen percent of the Islamic world. He's reaching over the heads of Arab governments to the Arab street, hoping to use these messages of Israel's destruction to rally support among the Sunni Arab masses."

The prime minister shook his head. "Something doesn't feel right. Iranians are not self-destructive. They are a nine-thousand-year-old civilization. And they know Israel has a lethal second-strike capability. This has to give them pause."

"How about China?"

"China? I think not. They are providing missile technology to Iran—no question. However, it isn't in Chinese interests to provoke a deadly holocaust in the Middle East that would impact their energy and oil interests."

"As you know, I always mistrusted Russia," Avram said.

"And not without good reason. But Russia remembers the Yom Kippur War of 1973; our missiles were pointed at the heart of Moscow. Maybe renegade ex-KGB officers or arms merchants are involved, but I don't read this as a strategic involvement at the Kremlin level. Ask yourself, Which power in the Middle East has the incentive and ability to develop the project, recruit and equip volunteers, provide the money, and sit back and watch the fireworks from a safe distance? Sound familiar?"

"Yes," Avram said. "Fifteen of the 9-11 hijackers were from Saudi Arabia."

"The split between Sunnis and Shiites is over a thousand years old. After the fall of Saddam Hussein's Sunni regime in Iraq, the political situation turned on its head. The Sunni minority in Iraq lost political power to the Shiites. The King of Jordan privately expressed his worries to me about the growing Shiite influence in the area. This concern increased after Hanoush was elected Iranian president. His nuclear ambitions pose a threat to the stability of all the

Gulf states. If a preemptive Israeli attack weakens Shiite Iran, what country will assume ascendency in the Middle East? Care to guess?

"The Saudis."

"Right. The Saudis never met a problem they didn't try to solve by throwing money at it. They keep you Americans happy by buying billions of dollars' worth of weapons they don't know how to use and airliners they don't need. In exchange, your country and the other western allies understand they'll have to protect Saudi Arabia to keep the oil and dollars flowing," he said tonelessly. "It's the way of the world, and everyone closes their eyes.

"If we can resolve this Iranian situation, or even imagine that Israel magically disappears—will the Sunnis and Shiites in Iraq suddenly start making love? Will the Sunnis, Shiites and Christians in Lebanon get together? Will it end the oppression of Christians in Egypt? Will it raise the status of women or put an end to violence as a political weapon in the Muslim world? It's a total illusion. What if the Saudis are playing a dangerous game and trying to draw Israel inextricably into it?"

"Then someone highly skilled is pulling the strings. King Abdullah?"

"No. Abdullah wouldn't dirty his royal hands. Sylvia Herzog had a meeting with his nephew, Prince Khalid in Washington. Khalid gave her a copy of a cable from Abdullah to the American president exhorting the U.S. to attack Iran and put an end to its nuclear program. The Saudi king asked the Americans to 'cut the head off of the snake,' but Khalid knows President Kennan will vacillate, so he made us an offer."

His housekeeper opened the door. "A call on your secure line. It is Mr. Bar-Lev."

"Chpindel here."

"We have a problem, Ephraim. The Muslim girl with the CIA who your friend Markus brought with him—she is wanted in England for multiple homicides."

"What the devil are you talking about, Gideon?"

"The picture of her taken at the airport was routinely forwarded to the Interpol database. Her photograph popped up immediately. She's wanted in London for the murder of the Iranian double agent and a hotel employee. There was a surveillance camera hidden in the lobby. She missed it."

"Oh my God."

"There's more, Ephraim. The killer's signature MO is one shot in the head and two in the chest; identical to the assassination of CIA Director Gervaise last week."

Chpindel was quiet, breathing deeply.

Bar-Lev added, "I've notified Washington. We will take her into custody."

"Be very careful, Gideon. The woman is an American citizen *and* a CIA agent. To our knowledge she has broken no Israeli laws. No SWAT teams. No reporters. Keep it quiet and controlled. This could become a nasty international incident. The sooner she is on a plane to the U.S., the better. Call me as soon as you have her safely in custody. And, Gideon, if she is everything you say, please be careful."

"Not to worry, boss. Talk to you soon."

Chpindel said, "That was Bar-Lev. It concerned your CIA associate."

"Agent Khouri. Is she all right?"

"I'm afraid the Muslim woman is what Mossad termed you— a *specialist*."

Avram's face turned ashen. "That's absurd. Who would make such an outrageous accusation, Bar-Lev? He hates Muslims."

"The British have Ms. Khouri on videotape shooting a London hotel clerk in cold blood a few minutes after the Zakariya fellow had been murdered upstairs in his hotel room; a professional job. The method of operation was the same as the assassination of your CIA director. One shot in the head and two in the heart. No shell casings found. Her signature, as it was."

Looking at Chpindel's dour expression, Avram knew it to be true. He felt deeply shaken; his breathing became rapid and shallow.

The prime minister added, "I worked with a Khouri in Iran years ago. Richard Khouri. He was CIA chief of station in Tehran. I wonder if there is any connection? The interesting question is, Why is the woman here in Israel at this critical time—and why did she come with you, Avram?"

...29

BAR-LEV RAPPED THREE TIMES. "Ms. Khouri. This is Gideon Bar-Lev. We met yesterday. Something has happened to Avram Markus; we need to talk to you."

After a long pause, he heard, "Just a minute, let me put something on."

Bar-Lev whispered to his two Mossad agents, "No rough stuff."

He heard the door lock click and a husky voice whispered, "You may come in now."

The Mossad director walked into the room followed closely by his men. A'isha Khouri stood in the backlit bathroom doorway wearing a filmy chemise nightgown. The beautiful woman stretched and the sheer gauze gown fell away, leaving her totally naked. The sight startled the three Israelis. They hesitated for an instant, and as they did, she swung her right arm up, moving so fast that they didn't see the gun, only the brilliant flash from the muzzle a moment before the bullet blew Gideon Bar-Lev's brains out. Then two more muted sounds from her 9 mm Beretta that recoiled slightly as neat puncture wounds materialized in the other two Mossad agents' foreheads.

She calmly closed the door, made a hasty phone call, dressed quickly, packed essentials into her shoulder bag, and took the stairs to the lobby, nodding pleasantly to the doorman. He was a tall, muscular, stiff-backed man in his middle fifties. Her skin prickled as she felt the man eyeing her suspiciously.

"Hey, you. Come back here," the doorman yelled.

Alie took a deep breath, fingering the Beretta in her handbag.

The big man lumbered toward her. "Go back and get a sweater, young lady. It's chilly today. You'll catch cold."

129

"I had my flu shot," she said, giving the doorman a wink and throwing a kiss. At the corner she hailed a cab. "Jerusalem Boulevard, Joffa."

Getting out at the Nouzha mosque, Alie paid the driver, carefully checked to insure she hadn't been followed, and walked quickly to a gray, nondescript Hyundai sedan parked across from the mosque.

"*Maa-salamah*," a male voice said. "Peace be upon you."

"That's even not funny, Blakeslee," she answered the tall, square-jawed, black CIA agent.

THE TELEPHONE CALL ARRIVED in the prime minister's office at 3 p.m. Chpindel snatched the receiver from the cradle after the first ring and brought it quickly to his ear. He could hardly recognize the sobbing voice on the other end of the line. It was Sylvia Herzog, Mossad's director of operations.

"Bad news, Mr. Prime Minister."

"How bad?"

Herzog answered the question to the best of her ability.

Chpindel closed his eyes and whispered, "My God."

MEIR RIVKIN DUG A CIGARETTE from his shirt pocket and lit it, cupping his hands. He had not slept in twenty-four hours, knowing Chpindel wouldn't let him rest until the crisis was over. Two high-powered laptops were plugged into full-size monitors; Meir was working both. He glared blearily at his screens and gave a sigh of resignation.

"Listen up," he groused. "This photo was taken of the *Samaria* in Kotka, Finland in 2008. Look for a ship with blue hull, yellow winches and a white bridge."

Esther Winer sat hunched over her computer. "I've checked the last five days of Ofek-7 recon photos over the Port of Bushehr. No sighting of this ship." The third mug of coffee was making her edgy; she had a mild hangover and was feeling lightheaded.

"Any luck at your end, Moshe?" Rivkin asked.

"Nothing. Nothing," Kasoff said, not bothering to look up from his screens.

A bell rang. "New satellite pictures of the Gulf are coming in," Esther announced as the photos began to roll off the computer transmission platen.

Rivkin slowly crushed out his cigarette. "These were taken one hour ago." The three huddled over the satellite images covering the Persian Gulf from the Strait of Hormuz to the Port of Bushehr.

"Esther, you start at the Strait of Hormuz; Moshe, you handle the area opposite Qatar. I'll work south from Bushehr."

"Look, Meir!" Esther said in a high-pitched voice, unable to contain her excitement. "It's the *Samaria*: a blue hull with yellow winches. Let me enlarge the satellite feed. Yes. See the name on the side?"

"What's her position?"

"I don't have coordinates. Looks like the *Samaria* is in the Gulf of Oman, a few miles south of the Strait of Hormuz."

Rivkin turned to Kasoff. "Calculate when the *Samaria* will arrive in Bushehr."

"The distance is 400 miles, Meir. Cruise speed for freighters of this class is approximately twenty knots—call it twenty-three miles per hour. The ship should hit the port by morning."

"Get Chpindel," Rivkin barked.

Esther said, "Tell the prime minister that there has been no unusual civilian or troop activity in Tehran or around the missile sites."

Meir Rivkin ignored her comments in his excitement.

THE PRIME MINISTER'S OFFICE WAS LOCATED at 3 Kaplan Street in the Kiryat Ben-Gurion section of West Jerusalem. Chpindel briefed Israel's president, Noa Aizenman, and returned to the building through the underground parking garage. Two body-guards followed him. He went directly up to the third floor conference room. Gathered together was his security staff: Uri Rubin, Ya'akov Agus, and Natasha Schleider. Sylvia Herzog stared silently out the window, her arms tightly wrapped around herself.

Uri Rubin rose and shook Chpindel's hand joylessly. Ya'akov Agus nodded solemnly. Melancholy seeped through Chpindel as he greeted Sylvia Herzog with a tight hug. Her large eyes were red and swollen. "Life goes on," he whispered. "I know you and Gideon were lovers—unprofessional, but human. Now you're head of Mossad." He studied her face. "I know you can do it."

"Everyone please be seated," Chpindel said as he settled behind his desk. "We are all aware of the tragic events of last night—"

"How could three armed Mossad men trying to arrest one woman turn into such a disaster?" Natasha Schleider grumbled.

Chpindel closed his eyes and shook his head.

"You don't know?" Schleider said, making no attempt to hide her irritation.

General Rubin started to interrupt her. "Let Natasha finish," Chpindel murmured.

Schleider persisted, "I'm sorry to have to say it, Ephraim. Under your watch, Mossad has screwed up more than this one operation. And where is your American friend? The Mossad deserter who brought Gideon's assassin to Israel?"

He raised his hands in a helpless gesture as he turned to the head of Shin bet. "Have your people find Markus, Ya'akov, before the old fool gets himself killed."

The prime minister's secretary buzzed. "Sir, Meir Rivkin—line one."

"Prime Minister." Rivkin's nasal voice came over the speaker-phone.

"Go ahead, Meir. We're listening."

"We located the Russian ship. The American was right; storms over the Atlantic delayed the vessel two days."

"Where the hell is it, man?" Rubin shouted into the speaker-phone.

"Entering the Strait of Hormuz as we speak. If the *Samaria* maintains her current speed, by dark she will be twenty miles out of the Port of Bushehr, still beyond the twelve-mile limit for Iran's territorial waters."

"Did you check the manifest?"

"In addition to millions of dollars worth of timber, the manifest lists five gas-powered water pumps loaded in Kaliningrad."

"Thank you, Meir, get some rest," Chpindel said quietly, ending the call.

Rubin exhaled loudly. "Ephraim, if the ship reaches Bushehr tonight, by tomorrow the bombs could be moved by rail or trucks anywhere in Iran. With your approval, we can prevent this. Shayetet 13 troops are standing by to intercept at sea."

"Get Halevi on the phone," Chpindel said.

In a matter of minutes the deep voice of the chief of the IAF, General David Halevi, came over the speakerphone. "Halevi here, Mr. Prime Minister."

"Do you understand your mission, David?"

"Yes, sir."

"Can you accomplish it?"

"What my men *can* do is their very best. We plan for contingencies. As you well know, sir, the unexpected can always bite you in the ass."

"What is your attack plan?"

"Our Night Raptor Squadron will handle the airlift. We will use two of the Yanshuf retrofitted UH-60A Sikorsky Black Hawk helicopters we got from the United States. With external fuel tanks we can carry 450 gallons on each inboard pylon and 230 gallons on each outboard pylon. This gives us an unrefueled self-deployment range of 1000 nautical miles—500 to target area and 500 back to base."

"How many men?"

"The UH-60A carries two pilots plus a crew chief-gunner. With the extra fuel tanks, we will carry eleven Shayetet 13 paratroopers per aircraft. Our plan is to close in darkness over the vessel and rappel our first team of eleven men. We will keep the second chopper in reserve. It will be dark; eleven men should be enough to get the job done."

Chpindel looked around the room. "Questions?"

Ya'akov Agus asked, "General, what will you do if you find bombs on board?"

"My instructions are to take control of the vessel and force the crew to head back down the Gulf until General Rubin notifies the Russians—"

Rubin cut in. "If news of their ship ferrying bombs to Iran becomes public, it will be an embarrassment for Moscow. We will notify Russia to take responsibility for the *Samaria*. Our objective will have been accomplished. An Israeli naval ship will be dispatched to pick up our people."

"Who will be in command?" Chpindel asked.

"I will fly the first copter," General Halevi said. "Captain Dani Aaronson will be the Shayetet 13 first assault team leader."

Rubin pressed him. "The green light, Ephraim. Do we go or not? Please! We are running out of time."

The prime minister felt an icy chill. For a moment longer, he hesitated. His eyes, normally clear pale blue, were red and tired. "Yes. The green light." Chpindel's voice was soft, nearly inaudible. "Go," he said. "Go."

...30

"WHAT WILL THEY THINK UP NEXT?" Meir Rivkin groused. "Rubin wants us to cyber-hack into the Saudi Arabian power grid, reprogram the Saudi Electricity Company computers to trigger a cascading blackout, and cut off all electricity for ten hours starting at 7 p.m. today."

Moshe Kasoff rushed in, breathless, waving a newspaper. Esther took one look, gasped and ran out of the room.

THE 6GS CELL PHONE CHIRPED, startling Avram. Chpindel's driver was taking him back to Tel Aviv. He picked up, but didn't speak.

"Avram. Avram. Is that you?"

Hesitantly he answered, "Yes?"

Esther stammered. "Your photograph and the CIA woman's are on all the TV channels and on every paper's front page. She is wanted for the murder of Bar-Lev and two Mossad officers. They are looking for you—as an accessory to the murders."

He felt a sharp stab of sudden anger. "Esther. Please do me a favor: find out all you can about a Richard Khouri. He was the CIA chief of station in Tehran years ago. Please get back to me as soon as you can. Thanks." He hung up.

Going back to the hotel for his suitcase was impossible. Police would be staking it out. Avram ran a quick mental inventory: his money, passport, credit card and driver's license were safely stored in his waist pack. At the city limits he thanked the chauffeur and hailed a taxi to the Arlozorov bus terminal on the southern part of Tel Aviv on Lewinsky Street. Avram sauntered into a nearby men's

135

store. He carried out his purchases in a plastic bag. At the Central Bus Station, Avram procured a ticket in his own name for Beer-sheba.

In the men's room he changed shirts, put on dark glasses, bunched his discarded clothes into a trash container, and lined up at the Shlomo Sixt car rental booth. Under the name F. Pierce, he rented an Opal sedan and asked directions for the route to Jerusalem.

Once on the road, Avram drove directly north towards Hertza-lea, turning east to catch route 90 towards the Lebanon border until he approached a huge hill of sand with an observation post on the Israeli side. At the Fatima Gate barricade, an Ethiopian girl in an Israeli Defense Force uniform checked each car that entered. She pushed sunglasses onto her forehead and studied Avram's passport carefully with practiced skepticism. Avram felt a sudden panic when the scrutinizing of his passport took longer than usual. The girl's eyes were dark and serious as she waved him through.

Driving into the town of Kfar Kila, he parked the Opal in a rough neighborhood. As in Fort Pierce, he left the keys in the ignition. Instinctively, his eyes flickered over the shaded doorways, the parked cars. He sat at an open-air sun-drenched terrace cafe and ordered an omelet, bread and a bowl of milky coffee. No one gave him a passing glance as he gazed south towards the place of his birth, Jezreel Valley.

...31

"HAVE YOU LOST YOUR MIND, SYLVIA?" Chpindel sputtered over the phone. "By what twisted stretch of the imagination did you contact the media and brand Avram Markus a deserter and a suspect in Gideon's murder? You know nothing about the man."

"I realize you served in the army together, but the facts are that Markus was a deserter from the IDF. And he was the person who brought Gideon's assassin into Israel."

"No, you fool. The American president was the one who authorized the two CIA officers' visit to Israel. Do you want to brand Kennan as an accessory also?" CLICK.

Herzog's face was crimson. She turned to her newly appointed director of operations, Ben Elazer. "There should be an age limit on prime ministers. The man is eighty years old and sick. He should retire. Now, what do you have for me?"

"We have been flooded with calls. A cab driver swears he took the Muslim woman from the Dizengoff area last night to Jerusalem Street in Joffa. We're combing the area and utilizing all of our connections. Nothing yet."

"How about Markus?"

"Markus has an everyman face, but we're narrowing down the leads. A cab driver thinks he drove him to the CBS terminal this morning. Time fits. Markus purchased a ticket in his own name for the 380 bus to Beersheba."

"Good. What else?"

"The Shlomo Sixt car rental agent at the bus station said a man looking like Markus rented a car in the name of Pierce. He asked directions to Jerusalem." Elazor added, "Beersheba's south, Jerusalem's east, so we presumed the old fox headed north."

"Agreed."

"By five-thirty we had notified all Israeli Defense Forces at northern border crossings. We faxed his photo and the rental car make, color and license tag number. A guard at the Fatima Gate barricade in Metullah remembered the car and the man's face." Elazer paused to take a breath. "Sometime late today, Markus crossed into Lebanon. He's gone."

THE SMALL VILLAGE OF GHAJAR straddled the Israel-Lebanon border. After walking four miles east, Avram stopped to rest, shaded his eyes and looked down at a blaze of whitewashed and pastel-colored buildings nestled on a plain of sun-bleached grass.

Looking back at Mount Herman, he recalled trying to explain to his son Zak that the snow-covered peak was called 'the eyes of the nation' because its high elevation made it Israel's strategic early warning station. Avram slowly continued his trek towards Ghajer, the town of Alawite Shiite Muslims, the town where Sarai and Zak had died, the source of the memories he carried like a constant pain. He felt achingly old. The black ghosts of his past had returned to haunt him.

Avram traveled the same footpath he had taken a half century earlier when he came to Ghujar to ask Sarai's Muslim father for her hand in marriage. He paused to watch a half dozen boys kicking a ball between the black-basalt boulders. Islamic music played from an old tape recorder. He recognized Sarai's family's beige stucco house wedged between the other cracked, graceless buildings that lined both sides of the narrow alley. A dog ran out from one of them, barking as Avram passed. Strips of colored plastic hung over the doorway. He knocked on the wooden door. A gray-haired man with a gaunt face and dark mustache opened the door and gazed at him warily.

In Arabic Avram said, "I'm Sarai's husband."

The mention of her name drew a sharp, querying look. The man made a clicking sound with his tongue; his brief smile vanished. A slight and wiry white-haired old woman appeared beside him in the doorway. Her clear brown eyes contrasted with a face lined with age and the harsh simplicity of her life. "Who is this stranger?" she demanded.

"Sarai's husband, the Jew."

She clasped her hands together. A film of tears came into the woman's eyes. "Ibrahim. Is you? *Ahlan wa salaam*, welcome to my home."

Avram bowed slightly, not knowing whether to offer his hand or not.

"Please," she said, opening the door wider. Avram followed them into a small sitting room. Black and brown tribal carpets covered the floor. The old woman insisted he sit on the worn pillows scattered across the carpet. The fragrance of mint tea filled the room. "I am Sarai's sister, Ramisa." Pointing to the man with the deeply-lined face, she said, "This is Danyal, my old goat of a husband." Tears again crept into the corners of Ramisa's eyes. She wiped them away with her sleeve and inhaled deeply. "After the... trouble, we never heard from you. We thought you dead."

He nodded. "I was traumatized over the *accident* and the government's clumsy attempt to cover it up. I deserted the army and fled to the United States—"

Danyal spat in disgust. His voice was guttural. "Jews go to America where the streets are paved with gold; we Muslims stay prisoners in Ghajar. Nobody gives a shit. Not the Syrians, Lebanese, Zionists, Hezbollah, nobody. Before the war we were Syrian nationals; then the Jews took the Golan Heights. They gave us Israeli citizenship."

His jawline tightened. "We live on the 'Blue Line' border; the politicians divided Ghajar and turned us over to Lebanon and the

UN. Now we are nothing but fucking Lebanese refugees, citizens of nowhere."

"Pay Danyal no mind," said Ramisa, clapping her hands and smiling. "Allah ordains your arrival. Tomorrow is our sacred Muslim holiday of *Eid al-Adha*."

The cell phone buzzed. Avram received a text message from Esther. He read it and then shook his head sadly.

FAR TO THE SOUTH, TWO UH-60A SIKORSKY HELICOPTERS of the Night Raptors Squadron took off from the squadron base in Beersheba. Twenty minutes later, in the fading sunlight over the Golan Heights staging point, General Halevi landed his lead copter. On command, twenty-six Shayetet 13 paratroopers ran for the choppers, dipped under their roaring rotors, and disappeared inside the two aircraft. Amid churning sand and dust, the choppers zoomed skyward.

General Uri Rubin phoned Chpindel. "The marine forecast is promising: diminishing winds, gentle seas with a slow moving front, and clear weather behind it. They're off."

IN THE NORTHEN SAUDI ARABIAN CITY of Turayf, lights started dimming and flickering in what appeared to be a power grid failure. The outage cascaded southeast to Rafha, then to Hafar al Batin and Al Jubay, located on the western side of the Persian Gulf. The president of the Saudi Electricity Company reported that the blackout in all the notheastern provinces was caused by a computer failure.

THE NIGHT RAPTOR SQUADRON HELICOPTERS flew across Saudi Arabian airspace. Captain Dani Aaronson watched his men rigging themselves into complicated harnesses.

"Attention!" Dani raised his voice over the noise of the aircraft to be heard. The thirteen members of his assault team concentrated on their team leader's words. All were in black: their faces, hands, watch caps, armored vests, guns, gloves, ropes, knives—all black. The gear had been checked, the weapons loaded.

"We have been over this plan a hundred times," Dani said. "This may be the most important assignment ever given a Shayetet 13 team. Our job is to rappel down to the *Samaria*, break into the captain's cabin, take control of the ship, round up all crew members, fight our way, if necessary, to the hold, and locate five metal containers possibly housing nuclear warheads."

He pointed to two men. "You'll come with me to the bridge. It is urgent we cut off outside communications immediately. Once we gain control of the vessel, collect all weapons and cell phones. We don't want Iranian patrol boats alerted. The trickiest part of the operation will be sliding down in the darkness with the possibility of armed hostiles firing up at us. Use stun grenades if you need to. If you fire your weapons, be careful of the warheads. The bomb casings should withstand small arms hits. If the bombs go off, we won't have to worry about a ride home."

There was hollow laughter.

"Any questions?" He studied the men. "No?" He gave a grim little smile. "Okay. Let's get the job done."

Clouds dominated the dark night. On General Halevi's ALR-69 radar warning receiver, he heard the steady beep of the Iranian radar beam sweep him every few seconds. On his screen he watched the images of four gunboats patrolling the rocky coastline fifteen miles away. Halevi knew each gunboat carried a Russian-made 37 mm gun mounted amidship. The lights of the Iranian coast flickered irregularly in the distance. "Five minutes to target area," Halevi said over the intercom.

Dani checked his watch. It was 17:00. The plan called for the assault team to unload at 17:05. He tugged once on the metal bit at his stomach through which the rappel ropes ran. He was conscious of the noisy *whup-whup-whup* of the rotors.

Over the intercom, General Halevi said in a voice calm and unemotional, "Approaching target, altitude 250 feet. I have a visual of figures gathering on deck. Sixty seconds and counting. God bless."

In the voice-activated mike suspended on its plastic arm inches from his lips, Captain Dani Aaronson shouted, "Commence operations!" He gave a quick visual sweep over the deck below him and heaved the long rope down. It disappeared, uncoiling into the darkness. Dani forced himself to take two deep breaths, gave a thumbs-up, and hurtled backwards into space. Twenty-five seconds later, he was the first to touch down. Like eerie black spiders descending from their webs, the Shayetet 13 assault team assembled and fanned out.

A shrill voice cackled over the *Samaria*'s loudspeaker in Russian. "Attention. All hands on deck to repel boarders."

"Flares," Dani ordered into his voice-activated mike. "We need visibility."

The air was suddenly filled with lighted flares hissing and popping. Dani could see clusters of crewmembers shocked and disoriented by the sudden attack. They huddled with stunned looks on their faces. From the bridge came shouting and yelling.

Moving cautiously, Dani took two men and headed up the companionway towards the wheelhouse. A large figure emerged in his path, a Russian sailor with a pistol. Dani shot him in the kneecap. The crewman fell to the floor cursing, his hands clutching the wound, blood pumping between his fingers. Dani climbed to the wheelhouse, surprising the three men inside as he entered the room with weapon raised. "Don't make problems," he said in Russian, "and nobody gets hurt." The captain was a broad-shouldered old man with white hair cut to stubble.

Dani pressed the public address button and announced, "This ship is under suspicion of transporting embargoed weapons. We will search the vessel and leave. You can then continue your voyage. Your cooperation is required. Thank you."

The armed response faltered. Crewman tossed down their weapons, muttering angrily. "Have you found the metal crates?" Dani asked over his headphone.

"Negative," came the response. "We've covered the top two decks so far. On the second deck we found S-300 anti-aircraft missiles and X-500 anti-ship missiles. We are working our way to bottom deck. It's slow. Armed crewmen are still wandering loose."

Dani left one trooper guarding the men on the bridge and raced down the stairwell three flights to the lower deck. Pushing open the door, he unhooked his Maglite and checked the room. In the corner he spotted five metal crates painted blue.

Standing in the shadows was a lone Russian crewman with cunning eyes, a cynical mouth and an AK-47. The man was an ex-Soviet Spetnez paratrooper who had served in Afghanistan. He had been drinking. Through the alcohol haze, the Russian saw a dark intruder with a gun and wearing body armor. He aimed at his head.

GENERAL DAVID HALEVI'S REPORT came over the speakerphone in the prime minister's office in bursts of static. Prime Minister Chpindel, Rubin, Agus, Sylvia Herzog, and Natasha Schleider hunched over the table, listening.

"Prepared to report on sea-interception mission, sir."

Chpindel took note of the chilly precision of Halevi's words. He shoved himself upright in the chair and with a trembling hand, set his coffee cup back in the saucer.

"Our people gained operational control of target vessel at 19:00 hours. On board were a quantity of Russian S-300 anti-aircraft missiles and X-500 anti-ship missiles. No nuclear warheads were located. I repeat, no bombs on board. The blue crates contained water pumps."

Cheers filled the room.

"You did it, Halevi," General Rubin shouted. "*Mazel tov.*"

Halevi continued his report: "In the operation, six Russian crewmen were killed, one wounded." He paused. The silence produced an awkward tension.

"It is with profound regret that I must inform you, Mr. Prime Minister, of the loss of Captain Dani Aaronson. He was killed leading the raid."

The room plunged into an ominous silence.

"Thank you, David," Chpindel finally managed to say. "Your men did well."

Uri Rubin looked at the prime minister. His face had gone shockingly white, the energy bled out of him. Chpindel started coughing, one hacking retch after another. And then collapsed.

PART III

JUDGMENT DAY

A Bedouin asked the Prophet Muhammad when the Judgment Day would occur. He said, "When the trust, al-amana, *is lost, then wait for Judgment Day."*

The Bedouin said, "How will it be lost?"

The Prophet Muhammad answered, "When power and authority comes in the hands of unfit persons, then wait for the Judgment Day."

Sahih Bukhart. Nawawi, #1837, Riyad as-Salihin

...32

IN PRESIDENT KENNAN'S BEDROOM the phone rang. Sleepily he glanced at the green fluorescent readout of the bedside clock: 1 a.m. "Kennan," he mumbled, half awake.

"Sorry to disturb you at this hour, Mr. President," Joseph Campbell said. "We just received word that Israel's Prime Minister Chpindel suffered a serious stroke."

"And what does that mean?"

"It means, sir, that today is November fifth, the day of *Eid al-adha*. It also means Natasha Schleider is acting prime minister. She is on record pushing for a preemptive strike against Iran. Now Schleider is the one with her finger on the button."

Kennan grimaced. "Shit. Shit. Shit."

"ON THE DAY OF EID AL-ADHA we honor Ibraham," Ramisa said to Avram. "For Muslims, Ibriham, 'Peace be upon him,' is the ancestor of Muhammad through his son Ishmael. He was obedient to Allah and not a worshipper of idols. In submission to Allah's will, Ibriham was willing to slay his son Ishmael, until it was revealed that Ibriham's sacrifice had been fulfilled. Following our exalted father's example, Muslims willingly sacrifice our own lives, or the lives of others, in submission to Allah's will."

"The sad fact, Ramisa, is that more people have been sacrificed in the name of Allah or God than for any other single reason in history." He took a deep breath. "As your brother-in-law, I pose to you a serious question. Answer me truthfully. If Israel was bombed on *Eid al-Adha*, would Muslims accept it as a sacrificial offering—and the will of Allah?"

She drew a sharp breath. "Impossible. It is unthinkable to contemplate such a tragedy occurring on *Eid al-Adha*. Today, Muslims around the world will attend prayers, enjoy their family and friends and exchange gifts. It is traditional today to visit a farm or make other arrangements for the slaughter of a sheep, camel or goat. One-third of the meat will be for family, one-third given to friends, and one-third is donated to the poor. The act symbolizes our willingness to sacrifice to help those in need. On the holiday of *Eid al-Adha* we open our hearts and share with others. Doing *anyone* harm today would defy the will of Allah." She smiled politely. "Dear brother. There are nonbelievers who would wage war against Allah and His messenger and strive to make mischief. Do not let them blind your eyes."

Avram recalled the prophetic words of a childhood refrain: *The world is full of kings and queens, who blind your eyes and steal your dreams.*

AVRAM'S PHONE CHIRPED. He listened to the strangled sounds of quiet sobbing.

"I had to call," Esther said. "Ephraim Chpindel had a stroke." Between teary gasps she also struggled to relay the tragic news of Dani Aaronson's death.

The double tragedy seized Avram's stomach in a vise. He closed his eyes and inhaled deeply. A lifetime of crisis experience took over, forcing him to concentrate on the immediate crisis. "Who is replacing Ephraim?"

"Natasha Schleider. She's called an emergency staff meeting in Jerusalem."

"What about the Russian ship and the bombs?"

"Meir telephoned. There were no bombs on the *Samaria*. Anti-aircraft and anti-ship missiles, but no nuclear warheads, thank God for that."

"Keep me informed, Esther." He killed the connection and turned to his sister-in-law. "Thank you, Ramisa, for removing my blindfolds."

Esther had explained that calls on his phone were encrypted, routed through proxies, and could never be traced. From memory, he punched in Dorothy Schreck's private line.

"Schreck here."

"Dot, it's Avram. Sorry I didn't get back to you sooner."

She paused. "I was worried. Are you OK?"

"I'm definitely not OK. The Israeli police are hunting me as an accessory in Bar-Lev's murder. The Khouri girl had us all fooled. Tell President Kennan that the Iranian threat did not materialize."

"Wonderful news. We heard Chpindel has had a serious stroke. Is that true?"

"That's what I was told."

Another pause. "Where are you, Avram?"

"In Kfar Kila, Lebanon," he lied. "I plan to slip back over the border at noon today for a final visit to the Neot Mordechai kibbutz cemetery. After that, I will try and find my way home."

"We have assets in the area who can help."

"Thank you, Dot. I'll be in touch."

"YOUR PICTURE IS ALL OVER CNN," said the vexed voice on Alie's cell phone.

"Couldn't be avoided. You wouldn't want me in custody, interrogated by Israelis," she replied icily. "Anyway, the mission is completed. Chpindel is out of the picture. I will be in Beirut tonight and fly to Riyadh tomorrow. Then we can discuss future arrangements."

"You must finish the other job first."

"Is that really necessary?" she fired back. "He's a harmless old man."

"No loose ends; he knows too much. And, Alie dear, never underestimate an experienced old fox like Markus. The guy may be old, but he has forgotten more than most agents learn in a lifetime. He will be at the Neot Mordechai kibbutz cemetery this afternoon at noon making his final farewells. Make sure it's *his* final farewell." Click.

...33

Russian Mystery Ship Hijacked in Persian Gulf

Manchester Guardian—November 5th. After undergoing repairs in Kaliningrad, Russia, the 4,000-ton cargo vessel *Samaria* set sail from Finland, carrying timber bound for Algeria. The *Samaria* was intercepted in international waters off the coast of Iran. Theories abound, including pirates and weapon smuggling. The Swedish newspaper *Metro* spoke by telephone with the *Samaria*'s captain. He said, "The pirates were dressed in black uniforms and seemed very professional. They spoke English, with some kind of accent."

David Osler, editor at *Lloyd's List*, maintained that the piracy theory did not fit, saying that modern-day piracy falls into one of three categories: the ship and crew are held for ransom, as often happens around the coast of Somalia; ships are re-sold; or captains and crews are held up for whatever cash is on board. He noted, "None of these applies, so you can rule out piracy. It must be some other form of crime."

Mikhail Voitenko, editor of Russia's *Sovfracht* maritime bulletin, noted that Kaliningrad is notorious as a smuggling haven specializing in the illegal transport of cigarettes, vodka and cars. The *Samaria* mystery also sparked speculation about a possible arms shipment destined for Iran. Russia dismissed reports that Russian missiles were on board. Moscow announced that the Russian navy recaptured the ship, killed the hijackers and rescued the crew.

A senior MI-6 figure close to Israeli intelligence told the BBC that Israel has been linked to the interception of the *Sa-*

maria. The British intelligence source said Israel had told Moscow it knew the ship was secretly carrying a Russian air defense system for Iran. There has been no official confirmation of the report.

...34

AVRAM LEFT FIFTY DOLLARS on the table, filled a bottle with water, and slipped quietly away while his in-laws were asleep. The sun slipped behind a bank of clouds as he followed the footpath from Ghajar south toward kibbutz Neot Mordechai. He planned to arrive at the gravesite before nine o'clock, early enough to study the terrain and stake out a tactical position.

After a tiring forty-minute uphill walk, Avram, puffing and short-winded, reached the kibbutz apple orchard. He spied his favorite apple, the Anna, a yellow variety with a red blush and sweet, crisp flavor. The Teva-Neot health shoe factory, where Sarai had worked, had been repainted white with a green roof. People were moving about the kibbutz, farm workers with sunburned faces and callused hands. Avram kept his hands in his pockets and his gaze lowered to the path in front of him as he passed the children's farm. He noted a shovel leaning against a tree and carried it over his shoulder.

At the well-tended cemetery he paused at the graves of his parents, buried beneath simple headstones. He laid a stone on each grave and recited the words of the mourner's Kaddish. He repeated the prayer for Sarai and Zak. Tears did not come. They never had. Anger and bitterness, but never tears. He glanced at his wristwatch: 10 a.m. Avram inhaled. Anger and bitterness were unnecessary distractions for what he intended to do.

He knew she would come through Kiryat Shemona, turn at Route 9977, and follow the road to Manara Cliff on kibbutz Manara. From there he expected Alie to leave her car and walk the rest of the way, off the road, to avoid detection. As a professional, she would choose a firing position with the western setting sun at her

153

back. Avram studied the tree line and settled on a location fifty yards away hidden by an outcropping of rocks. Without a hat, he was feeling dizzy from the sun and the long walk. He sipped water and waited patiently, musing, *They played me for an old fool.*

For one hour he waited, slowly moving his head from side to side, using the peripheral vision technique he had taught Mossad recruits. Suddenly, he sensed movement. A lone figure wearing a hooded coat cautiously edged towards the kibbutz cemetery. Two hundred yards away the dark figure stopped, paused, and then continued forward. *The rifle is under her coat*, he guessed.

The sniper selected a well-concealed firing position in the orchard.

Avram scanned the area, drew one more long breath, and started crawling forward on his belly. In the dry air the sky looked a dirty white. His back ached. His thigh felt tortured. The wind picked up, deadening sound as he snaked closer. A knife slipped from a sheath on his right forearm and fell into his right palm. *She knows the rules of the game. You can't live our kind of lives and expect to live forever.* Sweat poured from his forehead. Avram stifled a sneeze by pressing his left thumb hard against his nose. Focusing, he followed his habitual pre-kill routine, silently repeating the Sayeret Matkal mantra: *"Who dares wins. Who dares wins."*

As he edged across the final ten feet, the old assassin hesitated for the first time in his life. The hooded figure, alarmed by a noise or sensing a presence, swung around, pointing the rifle directly at Avram's chest. A finger tightened on the trigger.

Two quick spits from a silencer sounded softly, striking the sniper in the upper chest. Blood spurted as the man collapsed on the dry dirt.

Avram turned to face Alie Khouri holding a smoking 9 mm Beretta. Motioning with the tip of her gun at the body, she said, "It's Blakeslee Lane. Your girlfriend, Dot, doesn't like loose ends. Apparently, that includes me as well." She scrutinized Avram's heavy breathing. "Are you OK?"

"Goddamnit. Will everybody stop asking if I'm OK?"

"Other than that knife, are you armed?"

"No."

"Any deadly little creepy-crawly scorpions?"

He shook his head.

"Mossad reinforcements hiding in the apple trees?"

"Just me."

"Where is your killer-cane?"

"I traded it for a shovel."

"How convenient." She stepped in close and patted him down. "What's this?"

 "My cell phone."

"If it isn't some secret Israeli device that transmits and receives signals, keep it."

They sat in silence for a moment, looking at each other. A stranger might have mistaken them for a father and daughter. Finally, Alie smiled and said, "Were you really going to plunge that Swiss Army blade into my back?"

"I thought about it. One way or another, I came to say good-bye."

"We are more alike than you care to admit, Avram Markus. Christians in CIA Special Ops are Case Managers; Jews are Specialists, but Muslims are branded Islamic Assassins."

He permitted another silence to grow between them.

"You must wonder why I got involved in this nasty business."

Avram nodded.

Her eyes hardened. "I didn't choose this life; it was chosen for me. My family was murdered in 1979 when the Ayatollah's people overran the Tehran embassy. Khomeini's thugs set fire to our car. I was pulled out before the car was ripped apart by an explosion." She paused. "The last thing I remember about my parents is seeing them engulfed in a ball of flame."

"I'm sorry—"

She cut in, "The government sent me home to Michigan, to the tender, groping care of one foster family after another. I applied to the CIA. They couldn't turn me down; my dad's name is on the Agency's Wall of Honor. Like you, I became proficient at disposing of dirty laundry. Dorothy took a liking to me professionally and sexually. I earned this assignment the hard way."

"What assignment?"

"You were selected by Schreck to be the bait to get me close to your old comrade, Ephraim Chpindel. Schreck believed Chpindel would never permit Israel to launch a preemptive nuclear strike."

Avram looked confused. "Was I set up to pass on Zhukov's false information?"

Alie nodded. "General Zhukov was Dorothy's idea."

"Was she the mastermind of this insane plot?"

"No, it was above Dorothy's pay grade."

"Who?"

She shrugged. "This is only pillow talk. She told me that one of the Washington 'wise men,' whoever he is, has assurances that Natasha Schleider, as prime minister, would implement the Samson Option. Chpindel had to be disposed of. As it turned out, I didn't need you, because Dani Aaronson agreed to introduce me to his uncle. And now, with Chpindel in a coma, Schreck's plan is implemented." She paused to take a deep breath. "And mine as well: to revenge the pain of my parents' murder, to destroy the Iranian mullahs in their own hellish ball of flames."

"I understand pain. Mine lies buried under those gray headstones. Chpindel's pain was losing his nephew Dani during a raid on a Russian ship last night."

Alie's eyes widened in surprise.

"If Israel launches a firestorm," Avram continued, "I will have sparked it. There was no Iranian threat—this time." His tone was tinged with sorrow. He handed her Esther's cell phone. "Please read this text extracted from Mossad files."

CONFIDENTIAL MOSSAD REPORT: November 15, 1979

HaMossad leModi'in uleTafkidim Meyuchadim

The coup on August 19, 1953, resulting in the overthrow of the democratically elected Iranian Prime Minister Mohammad Mosaddegh, was instigated by the U.S. Central Intelligence Agency. The collapse of Iran's first democratically elected government ushered in a twenty-five year dictatorship under Mohammad Reza Shah Pahlavi, who relied heavily on U.S. weapons to remain in power until he was overthrown in February of this year.

For many Iranians, the coup exposed the duplicity of the United States presenting itself as a bastion of freedom while resorting to underhanded methods to overthrow Mosaddegh in furtherance of American strategic interests

The CIA reportedly bribed thugs, clergy, politicians and military officers to participate in the coup against Mosaddegh. On 19 August, a pro-Shah crowd, paid by the CIA, marched on the prime minister's residence. Mosaddegh was arrested, tried and convicted of treason by a military court of the Shah. On December 21, he was sentenced to solitary confinement in a prison cell in Tehran for three years and then placed under house arrest for the rest of his life.

Pahlavi ordered the execution of military officers and student leaders closely associated with Mosaddegh. Shortly thereafter, and with the help of the CIA chief of station and Mossad operatives, the Shah created a secret police force called SAVAK, which became infamous for its brutality.

Shah Pahlevi ruled until overthrown by a popular revolt in 1979. The actions of the CIA, and in particular the chief of station, Richard Khouri, are widely believed to be responsible for the 1979 Iranian revolution, which deposed Shah Pahlevi and replaced the pro-Western royal dictatorship with the anti-Western Islamic Republic of Iran.

ALIE SAT STILL AS A STATUE, legs folded beneath her. A single tear spilled onto her cheek. She punched away the tear, as if ashamed of her weakness.

"Let's get this over with," Avram said softly. "I'm not one to pass judgment on anyone's actions, yours or your father's. My hands have had blood on them—forever, it seems." He took a deep breath. "I am a Jonah. Death followed me my entire life." Ignoring her gun, he touched Alie's shoulder gently. "You know that you can't trust Schreck. Others, like Lane, will be dispatched to silence you. Go to Switzerland. Change your face and fingerprints; live your life." His shoulders slumped. He was bone-weary. His thigh ached painfully. "I'm worn out. My life started at Neot Mordechai. It is fitting it should end here."

Her eyes seemed a long distance off.

"I have a request." He smiled. "A last request, if you will. I ask that you take care of matters in a manner in which we are both familiar and then bury me next to my family. In many ways you remind me of my beautiful Sarai."

In a peaceful silence they sat for a long while without speaking.

"And in many ways," she said tenderly, "you remind me of my father. I'm sorry, my dearest Avram, that I will be unable to grant your final wish."

Before he could respond, Alie raised the Berretta to her temple. In one swift movement she pulled the trigger. The silenced handgun emitted little more than a whisper. Her eyes grew still, and then glazed. A'isha Khouri envisioned a ball of orange flames rising in the sky and heard her father calling her name as she slid to the ground. Then there was darkness.

"No!" Avram screamed, dazed, in shock. He fell to his knees in uncontrollable sobbing. For the first time in all those many years he cried, mourning his lost wife and son, grieving for Alie—the daughter he'd never had—and for all the unremembered faces of those he had killed working on the dark side of the CIA's dark service.

Avram lay prostrate for what seemed like an eternity. Slowly he rose, wiped his eyes, took the shovel, and buried the girl next to his family. He left no marking on A'isha Khouri's grave. He smoothed the dirt and covered it with branches from his favorite Anna apple tree.

Taking the shovel, he buried the CIA man in a shallow grave fifty yards away. Not wanting to chance crossing the border again, Avram took the car keys and all identification from Agent Blakeslee Lane's pocket and buried them a distance away. He drank a deep draft of water and started walking slowly north, back towards Ghajar, Lebanon. Tiredness engulfed his body. But he kept walking, for his mind refused to rest.

...35

THE COMMITTEE OF HEADS OF SERVICES met in the prime minister's office in Jerusalem. Joining Natasha Schleider were Lt. General Uri Rubin, Ya'akov Agus, and Sylvia Herzog, acting chief of Mossad.

"Ephraim is in critical, but stable condition in the Sheba Medical Center," Schleider said. "He suffered a massive brain hemorrhage."

"What's the prognosis?" asked Uri Rubin.

Schleider shook her head. "At this stage the doctors won't say. Ariel Sharon was in a coma for years. In any event, Ephraim is seriously incapacitated. I am legally empowered to serve as interim prime minister for up to one hundred days. After that, if Ephraim is permanently incapacitated, we will have new elections. Anyone have a problem with that?"

There was complete silence.

"Bring us up to date, Uri."

"The Russians clammed up. If it weren't so serious, it would be laughable to believe this fuss was over a load of timber. The Kremlin claims a rescue mission involving destroyers and submarines boarded the *Samaria*, killed the hijackers and saved the crew. Fortunately there were no warheads on board, but we can't ignore the fact the ship also contained advanced anti-aircraft weaponry destined for Iran. Hanoush is a fanatic. We ignore him at our risk."

Sylvia Herzog spoke, her eyes icy cold. "Here is what Hanoush said last week." She put on glasses. " 'God willing, we shall soon experience a world without Zionism.' "

"I don't believe in sitting around while others plot our destruction. When Hanoush talks about wiping us off the face of the earth,

160

I, for one, take him at his word. We lost too many in the first holocaust; we cannot afford to lose our nation in a second one—at least not without a struggle."

Schleider looked questioningly at Ya'akov Agus. The head of Shin bat took a moment to organize his thoughts before answering. "I do not believe there is some grand pan-Arab plot against us. Egypt, Tunisia, Libya and Bahrain have too many other things to worry about. I do recognize specific threats, like Hamas, Hezbollah, Al Qaeda, and our immediate concern with Iran. It is true Iran has obtained the capacity to launch an attack upon us. Having the capacity and actually doing it are two different things. No nuclear bombs were found on the Russian ship."

Ya'akov's tone grew quiet. "The founding of Israel was a miracle, and except for our policies in the West Bank, something to be proud of. I prefer the route of diplomacy, rather than seeing Israel dragged into the abyss by launching a preemptive attack on innocent Iranians—"

Sylvia Herzog cut in. "But Ya'akov, most Middle East leaders agree that Iran should be neutralized." She quoted from another document in her hands: "King Abdullah of Saudi Arabia asked the United States to 'cut off the head of the snake.' He is on record requesting an attack on Iran, putting an end to their nuclear weapons program. Prince Khalid told me many other Middle East leaders feel the same way."

Agus shook his head. "No, Sylvia. Those leaders will not speak out publicly. They will celebrate in private any triumph over the hated Persians. But publicly, they would join with their people in the streets to condemn Israel if we carried out an attack."

"Listen to me, people," Rubin said. "We are a one-bomb state. Israel cannot tolerate the human or economic disaster that would result from a single low-yield nuclear explosion. This is a scenario that could bring our nation to its knees."

He nodded to Schleider. "I recognize that ordering a preemptive nuclear strike is the hardest decision any leader is called upon to make. Harry Truman understood that when he approved bombing Japan. But the longer we wait to attack, the more enriched uranium the Iranians will have. The window for military action is sliding closed. The Iranians have dragged out the diplomatic process for precisely that reason. We have to do something."

"What are you proposing?"

Rubin pulled up a chart and placed it on the table for everyone to see. "The orange arcs represent Jerico III missiles to be launched against the uranium enrichment plant in Natanz, the heavy water facility in Estahan, and the nuclear research centers in Bushere and Arak." He paused. "The red lines represent follow-up strikes by our air force using the southern route through Saudi Arabia. Sylvia received route authorization direct from the Saudi ambassador in Washington. All IDF forces have been placed on alert."

Natasha Schleider's face shed any remnant of color. This was not the kind of awesome responsibility she had anticipated when she entered politics. "It was Netanyahu who said that if the Arabs put down their weapons today, there would be no more violence, but if the Jews put down their weapons today, there would be no more Israel."

She took off her glasses and rubbed her eyes. "Hanoush is like Hitler; it's the '30s all over again. Everyone knew Hitler was a problem, yet the Western powers sacrificed Czechoslovakia to avoid confrontation. Had the West preempted against Germany, there would have been a lot of controversy and a lot of argument. But six million Jews would have been saved. And it's the same thing today with Iran."

She looked around the room. "We cannot permit Israel, the birthplace of our dreams, to become the graveyard of Zionism. I would like a... show of hands," she mumbled nervously. "Who goes along with the plan that Israel should launch our missiles in a preemptive strike against Iran's nuclear facilities? Please raise your hands."

Rubin and Sylvia Herzog looked at each other hesitantly; they lifted their hands.

"And you, Ya'akov?" Schleider asked.

"It appears to me my friends who voted to attack Iran see nothing but perpetual war or the threat of war. Do you realize that Natanz is a city of forty thousand people, and Arak has five hundred thousand? And Isfahan is the second largest city after Tehran, with a population of three million. Are we Jews willing to initiate a holocaust in Iran—to have people cremated alive or poisoned by radiation released from nuclear rubble? There is no way the world would idly stand by and watch as we drop a nuclear weapon in the vicinity of so many people. Why have a state at all? Why not go somewhere safer and hope to be a protected minority, like the Jews in America? I vote no."

Natasha Schleider made a church steeple of her forefingers and pressed it to her lips, trying to regain her composure before responding. She took off her glasses and wiped them. Finally the interim prime minister took a deep breath. "The history of mankind began in the Middle East," she intoned quietly. "And it will probably end there too, but not on my watch. Uri, order your troops and missile launchers to stand down."

...36

ON THE FLIGHT FROM BEIRUT'S Rafic Hariri Airport to New York, the Air Canada stewardess remarked to the pilot, "The passenger in window seat 24 refuses all offers of food or beverage. I have tried communicating in English, French and Arabic, but the old man ignores me; he just stares out the window."

After the flight landed at Kennedy Airport, the passenger activated an unusual-looking cell phone and placed two local calls: one in Hebrew, one in Russian. Avram took an airport bus to Penn Station, walked slowly over to 6th Avenue, and entered the small, musty bookshop, Judaica Treasures.

"*Shalom*," the proprietor said. "A pleasure to see you so soon again, sir."

Avram took out his wallet. "Do you take Visa, Irving?"

"You mean the Visa card I forged for you?" Irving snickered. "That's a good one." He went into the back room and returned with a hickory cane and a plastic bag. In a hushed whisper Irving said, "The cane has your custom built-in feature." He held open the bag for Avram to view the contents. "As you ordered: a 9 mm Beretta and an old Tokarev-33 semi-automatic pistol, with 9 mm Ultra cartridges; both wiped clean with an acid wash."

THE RUSSIAN BATHS SMELLED GAMEY AND MUSKY. Two ceiling fans stirred the heavy air. The spa employee with thick forearms and a dark beard was in animated conversation with Pyotr Zhukov's burly bodyguard.

"Is Zhukov in the Russian sauna?" Avram asked.

The surly attendant winked at Zhukov's man. "What goes on in the Russian baths stays in the Russian baths. Pay up or get lost, old man." The words were hardly out of the attendant's mouth when four rigid fingers jabbed into his solar plexus. The big man was taken by surprise, grunting in pain. Avram followed with a short straight fingertip blow just below the ear. The man's head jerked up and his mouth fell open. He crumpled onto the marble floor.

Zhukov's bodyguard was a lumbering giant. He took a knife from his pocket, slashed it in the air in front of him and lurched forward. As he did, Avram swung his hickory cane into the man's windpipe so sharply that he cracked the bodyguard's Adam's apple. The man's face turned purple; his eyes bulged. He dropped the knife, clutching at his throat with both hands. Avram heard the bodyguard's ragged but futile attempt to breathe as the huge man collapsed.

Avram put a glove on his right hand and pushed open the door to the sauna. He could barely see into the misty, rock-walled room. Intense heat seared his lungs. A dozen people huddled on the stone benches wreathed in a two-hundred-degree fog. In the far corner he spotted the bald, squat, powerfully built Mafia boss.

Zhukov stared in shock. He shrugged his shoulders, as if mystified at seeing Avram fully clothed. As the former Russian general started to rise, Avram fired twice, the double tap of a trained killer. Both shots struck the heart. People screamed as Zhukov tumbled forward onto the sauna floor. Avram stood over him, firing one more shot into the head. He tossed the Tokarev pistol into the icy pool and walked out.

When questioned by police, none of the dozen witnesses could say more than it was hard to see in the Russian sauna; the killer was quite unremarkable-looking; and he walked with a cane in his left hand. The sullen deskman was even less forthcoming. The police assumed it was a Mafia hit. An old Russian pistol without prints, found in the pool, was the murder weapon. A file on the case was opened, but never closed.

...37

THE PHONE IN HER LIBRARY RANG. "Schreck here."

"We need to talk."

A pause. "It wasn't personal. It was business. You *do* understand, don't you?"

"Yes. I do. And Blakeslee Lane is dead—a collateral casualty."

Schreck sounded like she had been drinking. "Congratulations."

He sighed deeply. "I'm sorry to have to tell you—Alie is also dead."

Avram heard an involuntary groan followed by silence. He thought the connection had been severed. After several moments, Schreck came on the line and said in a low voice tinged with alcohol, "When I joined the Agency they told me, 'You're not in the Girl Scouts, Dorothy. If you wanted to be in the Girl Scouts, you should have joined the Girl Scouts.' Life goes on. Right?"

He ignored the question. "Who was the architect of your bomb scheme?"

"And if I tell you, what do I get in return?"

"A chance to resign, collect your pension and live out your life quietly."

Another long silence. "And if I refuse?"

"I will hunt you down and kill you."

THE FRONT DOOR WAS UNLOCKED. Books lined the chocolate painted walls; a Wolf Kahn original hung over the fireplace.

"You shouldn't leave your door unlatched at night. It's not safe."

Schreck's eyes locked on Avram. "Crime is down in the District seventeen percent this year. Can I offer you a drink? The merlot grape is a close cousin to Cabernet Sauvignon in many respects. It is lower in tannins—"

He interrupted. "You are aware that hundreds of thousands of lives would have been lost if Israel had launched their missiles."

"Don't lecture me, please."

"Did you order Alie to murder Zakariya?"

Schreck took her time answering. She poured herself another glass of wine and nodded. "Part of the grand plan."

"Chpindel thought that Saudi Arabia was behind your plot."

She shook her head. "Prince Khalid pulls strings and bribes people, but the Saudis haven't the balls to get their hands dirty. They pay others for that privilege."

"*Others* like who?"

Schreck got up and locked and latched the front door. Then she drew the curtains facing on to Lowell Street. Whatever effect the wine had had was gone.

"This goes high, Avram, very high." Her face was drained of color. "It's not publicly known, but Kennan has Parkinson's disease. At the last meeting in the Situation Room, his shaking was more pronounced than ever. He will not seek another nomination. C. J. Landry will be the next Democratic presidential nominee. The polls show he can't overcome a Republican challenge. The polls also indicate forty percent of Americans believe the world will end at Armageddon. For that to happen, Israel must be protected. That forty percent includes a hell of a lot of right-wing, low and middle class, white, elderly, religious voters: the base Landry needs."

Avram narrowed his eyes. He listened intently.

"The vice president agreed with our CIA assessment. With Iran marginalized, we would regain Middle East dominance and head off the Chinese. Landry didn't believe we could afford the cost in blood and dollars of another American military adventure in the area. He wanted the Israelis to handle the job, but he didn't trust Chpindel. Landry wanted him removed."

"Did he also want Gervaise murdered?"

"You might call that my own career-enhancement plan to break through the CIA's glass ceiling. Landry sanctioned it. Phillip was greedy. He amassed a fortune covering up the Saudis' 9-11 mess. Internal Revenue was getting close to his offshore accounts. Gervaise's exposure would have given the Agency another black eye that we didn't need. We are a large, fossilized bureaucracy. Some of the people are mediocre at best. Most case officers don't speak the language of their subject countries. All they do is look at satellite photos and telephone intercepts. But many of our analysts are competent professionals. If the administration had listened to us about Iraq or Afghanistan, the results might have been different."

"May I use your bathroom?"

Schreck motioned with her head. "Through the dining room, just off the kitchen."

Avram closed the bathroom door and removed a glove from his pocket, placing it on his right hand. He reached into his waistband and withdrew the 9 mm Beretta. When he returned to the living room, Schreck turned to face him. She was looking squarely into the muzzle of the gun.

"Permit me to a share the story of the scorpion and the frog. One day a scorpion arrives at the bank of a river. He wishes to cross, but there is no bridge. The scorpion asks a frog sitting nearby if he would take him across the river on his back. The frog refuses, saying, 'I will not, because you will sting me.' The scorpion replies, 'It would be foolish for me to sting you because then we would both drown. I promise you safe passage.' The frog accepts the scorpion at his word and agrees to carry the scorpion across. But when they are halfway across the river, the scorpion stings the frog. The stunned frog asks, 'Why did you sting me? Now we will both die!' The scorpion replies, 'Because I'm a scorpion, and that's what scorpions do.'

"We are spies, Dorothy. We lie for a living. You *do* understand; it isn't personal." He fired two bursts into Schreck's chest and one in her brain, duplicating the murder of Gervaise. He turned off the lights, left the house, and drove to Reagan National Airport.

Dorothy Schreck's body was discovered the next morning when her cleaning lady came in for work. Police questioned neighbors on both sides of Lowell Street. No one had seen or heard anything. The police compared the killing to the assassination of CIA Director Phillip Gervaise and to the murder in London of Herro Zakariya by A'isha Khouri. They concluded that the MO's were similar: in both cases, a person known to the deceased had been admitted, because there was no sign of a forced entry; both victims were shot two times in the heart and once in the head; and no shell casings were found.

Local police and FBI agents were engaged in a nationwide search using photographs of the beautiful assassin. A file on the case was opened and never closed.

AFTER LANDING IN THE PALM BEACH AIRPORT, Avram punched in Esther Winer's pre-programmed number.

"You miss me already?" She chuckled.

"Esther, I need a big favor."

"Have I ever denied you *anything*?"

"Can you reverse your program that enlists other search engines to do the work and transmit information instead of collecting it?"

"What kind of information?"

"I need to plant information: Prince Khalid bin Abdul Al-Aziz of Saudi Arabia had secret meetings with Al Qaeda operatives to plan the overthrow of the Saudi king."

"I could create a few blogs to get the word out. After this, you'll owe me one." Then in a throaty whisper Esther Winer added, "Or maybe two or three, Tiger." He heard her giggling as she disconnected the call.

...38

Vice President Landry Suffers Heart Attack

Washington Post—Vice President C.J. Landry was visiting a homeless shelter, the Transitional Housing Corporation on 16th Street, for a pre-Christmas party when he apparently suffered a severe heart attack. The vice president was pronounced dead upon arrival at George Washington University Hospital.

C.J. Landry and his staff helped THC plan a holiday event for all seventy-nine families and other needy homeless individuals in the Washington metropolitan area. THC's residents, along with the vice president, sang Christmas carols, and each resident received a gift from Landry.

The last gift recipient greeted by the vice president before his fatal heart attack was an elderly homeless man with a cane and a pronounced limp.

The vice president's body will lie in state in the Capitol Rotunda, but the funeral will take place in the Georgia Hill Country that he called home.

...39

EPHRAIM CHPINDEL DIED IN HIS SLEEP a few days shy of the legal limit of one hundred days. Israel's president, Noa Aizenman, reappointed the Likud party, which Aizenman believed had the best possibility of creating a strong and stable coalition. Likud's newly elected leader, Ya'akov Agus, succeeded Chpindel as prime minister. Agus immediately picked Natasha Schleider, leader of the Yisrael Beiteinu party, as his deputy prime minister.

On Israeli television, Agus addressed the nation. "It is with sadness that I announce the death of our prime minister, Ephraim Chpindel, who died this morning in Sheba Medical Center. As a decorated soldier and recipient of the Medal of Honor, Ephraim was admired; as a leader of our nation and as a statesman, he was praised."

Ya'akov Agus' voice quivered with emotion. He paused to regain composure. "As my comrade in Sayeret Matkal and as my friend for half a lifetime, I will dearly miss Ephraim. Now it falls to all of us who love peace and all of us who loved Ephraim Chpindel to carry on the struggle. He cleared the path. And his spirit continues to light the way; light the way for all leaders of the Middle East to work together to insure that our children will inherit a future of hope and true security.

"Let me say to all Israeli citizens: even in this hour of darkness, Ephraim's spirit lives on. Look at what you have accomplished: making a once-barren desert bloom, building a thriving democracy in a hostile terrain, winning battles and wars... and now we must win the peace which is the only enduring victory."

A WHILE LATER, IN AN INTERVIEW with the international media, the subject of Iran's nuclear capability was raised. Agus said, "The Jewish people and the Iranians have a long and common history. It is a history that has been overwhelmingly positive until recently. It is time for both nations to stop waving around the scarecrow of threats and refrain from making belligerent statements. We desire peaceful relations with Iran without preset conditions and ultimatums. However, until Israel's security is assured, the Samson Option will be preserved. The meaning of our watchword, 'Never Again,' implies first and foremost that Jews will never again go quietly and submissively to our deaths."

The following morning, in a quiet ceremony, Ephraim Chpindel was buried in the cemetery located on the northern slope of Mt. Hertzl, known as Helkat Gedolei Ha'Uma, the burial ground allocated for leaders of the state of Israel and for soldiers fallen in the line of duty. Ephraim Chpindel was buried next to his nephew, Captain Dani Aaronson.

IN WASHINGTON, PRESIDENT THOMAS KENNAN announced he would not seek reelection. Details of his illness were leaked to the *Washington Post* from an unnamed source at Bethesda Naval Hospital. Kennan's hand tremors and slurred speech patterns were diagnosed as symptoms of advanced Parkinson's, a progressive, incurable brain disorder.

In the ensuing primary campaign, former Secretary of State Dr. Cassia Politto emerged as the front-runner for the Democratic Party nomination. A flurry of polls showed that Politto drew strong support from Hispanic, black, Catholic, and college-age voters, in addition to labor unions and women of all political stripes.

The presidential tracking poll *Rasmussen Reports* reported 73 percent of Americans considered terrorist attacks as their major concern. Dr. Politto announced that, if nominated, her choice for vice president would be former Chairman of the Joint Chiefs of Staff

Admiral Jeb Baysinger. Baysinger's experience as chairman of the Joint Chiefs was comforting to security-conscious voters; his staunch support a few years earlier for the 'Don't ask, don't tell' repeal garnered support from gay rights advocate groups.

A CNN Opinion Research Corporation survey tracking the race for the Republican nomination reported that the field of possible contenders appeared wide open, with no front-runner. Republican strategists urged the party to continue sanctifying tax cuts and demonizing spending and to use the growing anger over citizenship rights as a wedge issue against Dr. Cassia Politto's projected candidacy.

Interviewed on Fox TV, popular author and evangelist Dr. Isaiah Bowman said, "I don't believe in giving children of illegal immigrants who enlist in the military a path to citizenship, just because they are willing to die for their country. Also, the atheists, Muslims and anybody else who doesn't believe in Jesus should never be considered as true American citizens. After all, this is one nation under God."

...40

Saudi Ambassador to U.S. Reported Missing

The New York Times—Reports out of Riyadh allege Saudi Arabia's former ambassador to Washington, Prince Khalid bin Abdul Al-Aziz, has been arrested for plotting a coup to try and ensure the kingdom would continue under the rule of the Sudairi branch of the Al Saud family.

According to Saudi opposition sources, Prince Khalid is being held in Dhaban Prison in northwest Jeddah, a high-security jail where terrorist suspects and political opposition figures are imprisoned.

Since his return to the kingdom from Washington in December after his 22-year stint as ambassador, Khalid has not been seen in public. The last official sighting was in December, when he met privately with the king in Jeddah.

In the months before his disappearance he traveled frequently to Moscow, both to negotiate arms deals and to try to persuade the Kremlin to halt its military cooperation with Iran. There has been speculation his activity in Russia could be connected to his disappearance: a stream of worldwide blogs claim Khalid's abortive coup was exposed by Russian intelligence.

Wherever Prince Khalid bin Abdul Al-Aziz is now, his glory days are past—unless another of his patrons becomes king.

...41

AVRAM'S CELL PHONE CHIRPED. He picked it up without speaking.

"Avram, dear. How are you? This is Esther."

"Hello."

"I have exciting news. I received a job offer from East Coast Electrical Security Company. The company specializes in electronic countermeasure security systems. And they are located in Port St. Lucie. Isn't that near where you live?"

"About thirty minutes away."

"What do you think about my taking the job?"

"What does Shaul think?"

"Shaul is thinking with his pecker. He found a soulmate at Princeton, a twenty-year-old blonde *shiksa* graduate student."

Silence.

"I was wondering, Avram dear, could you help me find somewhere to stay?"

"You can bunk with me for a while. I have an extra bedroom."

"Wonderful," Esther breathed into the phone. "We can use it for guests."

AT 3 A.M., THE FORT PIERCE black and white police patrol cruised slowly past the library and Indian River Lagoon waterfront park. Instead of the normal complement of two officers, budget cuts mandated one officer per car. The patrol car driver noticed that the old guy with the cane was back, but his limp was hardly perceptible. The man smiled and waved his cane at the officer, who muttered, "The old bird seems to be in a jovial mood—probably drunk."

175

...Epilogue

STARTING WITH AN UNKNOWN BLOGGER in Australia, the legend first hit the Internet. The story spread when a supermarket tabloid in America reported an exquisitely beautiful Muslim woman was a modern-day assassin. *Rolling Stone Magazine* created a sensation by publishing a feature article entitled "The Legend of Queen A'isha."

The media offered no more than the vaguest descriptions of the female assassin until a British paper, the *South London Press*, released, without authorization of Scotland Yard, a video on YouTube picturing her killing a desk clerk in a London hotel lobby.

CNN enhanced the story, adding, "To date the mysterious, elusive A'isha is reported to be the main suspect in 150 unsolved murders worldwide, including the shooting of a London hotel employee; the murders of an Iranian, Herro Zakariya; three Israeli Mossad officers; and the American CIA Directors Schreck and Gervaise."

Middle Eastern newspapers and television continued the narrative. In the Sunni-dominated countries of Egypt, Jordan, Saudi Arabia and Syria, Muslims believed their legendary Queen A'isha had returned from the ashes to lead the faithful against the Shiites. According to *Charisma,* Egypt's leading magazine, A'isha was the most powerful woman in Islamic history, the one who commanded troops after Muhammad's death in the first Islamic civil war and set into motion the division of Islam into Shiite and Sunni sects.

In the mosques and state-controlled media of Iran, Shiite Muslims were warned by the mullahs that the woman called Queen A'isha, born in seventh-century Mecca, was a Sunni Muslim contemptuous of the prophet Muhammad's family. They preached that the person mentioned on the *Al-Alam* News Network and *Al-*

Kawthar TV was a fictitious creation of the Zionists to stir up another *fitnah*—another Islamic civil war.

Over the years, the French-based Interpol, Scotland Yard, the FBI, and police organizations of most major Middle Eastern nations opened files on the assassin, Queen A'isha. None were ever closed.

LaVergne, TN USA
21 March 2011
220892LV00002B/5/P